*Jack kept reviewing his meeting with Johnny.
Would his son heed his advice?*

He suspected not. The kid was blinded by a mind-set that would have been justified had the underlying premises been true. But of course, he didn't know they weren't.

Margaret had argued that Jack ought to spell out what had really happened twenty-five years ago. The trouble was Johnny wouldn't believe him. As for the diaries, maybe Margaret was right. There was a lot to be said for allowing Johnny to read them. The boy would learn the truth, but at what price?

Better let him keep his fond memories of her, Jack concluded, even if they were falsely based.

He ought to get some sleep. Tomorrow was going to be a big day, an important day. A milestone. A turning point. How would he measure success? By winning the NASCAR NEXTEL Cup Series championship? Or by losing it?

Dear Reader,

Every culture, it seems, has its counterculture. If you play soccer, you probably don't play football. If you're a horse person, you probably ride Western or English, not both. Maybe it's because they're closely related but distinctive, or because having skill in one doesn't always translate into skill in the other.

Take auto racing, for instance. There are rallies and drag races. Stock cars and Formula One cars. And never the twain shall meet. Well…except maybe at Infineon Raceway, where stock cars race on a winding road course—clockwise.

So here I am, playing the what-if game again. What if a world-famous Grand Prix driver decided to take on the world of NASCAR? And what if his chief rival was his own father? The generation gap. Age and experience versus youth and impetuosity. Hmm…

I mean, it's not as if such things never happen.

I hope you've been enjoying Harlequin's officially licensed NASCAR series as much as I have.

I'm always glad to hear from readers, and I'll be particularly anxious to get your reaction to this story and the NASCAR series in general. You can write me at P.O. Box 61511, San Angelo, TX 76904-9998. See you at the races.

Ken Casper

NASCAR

MILES APART

Ken Casper

TORONTO • NEW YORK • LONDON
AMSTERDAM • PARIS • SYDNEY • HAMBURG
STOCKHOLM • ATHENS • TOKYO • MILAN • MADRID
PRAGUE • WARSAW • BUDAPEST • AUCKLAND

ISBN-13: 978-0-373-21781-6
ISBN-10:   0-373-21781-1

MILES APART

Copyright © 2007 by Harlequin Books S.A.

Kenneth Casper is acknowledged as the author of this work.

NASCAR® and the NASCAR Library Collection are registered trademarks of the National Association for Stock Car Auto Racing, Inc.

KEN CASPER,

aka K. N. Casper, figures his writing career started back in the sixth grade when a teacher ordered him to write a "theme" explaining his misbehavior over the previous semester. To his teacher's chagrin, he enjoyed stringing just the right words together to justify his less-than-stellar performance. That's not to say he's been telling tall tales to get out of scrapes ever since, but...

Born and raised in New York City, Ken is now a transplanted Texan. He and Mary, his wife of thirty-plus years, own a horse farm in San Angelo. Along with their two dogs, six cats and eight horses—at last count!—they board and breed horses and Mary teaches English riding. She's a therapeutic riding instructor for the handicapped, as well.

Life is never dull. Their two granddaughters visit several times a year and feel right at home with the Casper menagerie. Grandpa and Mimi do everything they can to make sure their visits will be lifelong fond memories. After all, isn't that what grandparents are for?

You can keep up with Ken and his books on his Web site, www.kncasper.com.

To Florence and Jack Domin
Who've been there through thick and thin
For more than sixty years.
You've inspired more than you realize.

ACKNOWLEDGMENT

None of this would have happened without
Marsha Zinberg and Tina Colombo.
Thank you for your confidence and support

CHAPTER ONE

JACK SLAPPED HIS GLOVES on the table and stomped over to the refrigerator. He needed to shuck his driving uniform, get under a cool shower and scrape the grime off his sweaty body. But first he needed a drink. A two-and-a-half-hour, four-hundred-mile race left him as dehydrated as a prune. He grabbed a lime-flavored sports drink, twisted off the cap and drank so greedily some of the green liquid dribbled down the sides of his mouth. At the moment he didn't care.

He'd gone into this last race of the season with high hopes after winning the number three position in the qualification round on Friday afternoon. His car, Number 424, had been running in top form. Everything seemed set for Victory Lane and the NASCAR NEXTEL Cup Championship, and he needed a win badly. His last two seasons hadn't gone especially well, to the point where pundits were beginning to wonder if Jack Dolman, three-time NASCAR NEXTEL Cup Champion, might be getting ready to hang it up. At fifty he was an old-timer in a sport that saw most of its players in their twenties and thirties.

No, dammit, he wasn't ready to call it quits, not yet.

He'd been racing cars of one sort or another for forty years. As far as he was concerned, they'd have to pry him out from the driver's seat and probably bury him with the steering wheel still clutched in his cold, dead fingers. But simply being an "also ran" wasn't good enough. It never had been. He had to win. That was why he raced.

He heard footsteps coming down the aisle of the 18-wheeler between the tool bins toward the lounge. Haulers were off-limits to reporters, but occasionally one, usually an eager novice, would violate the rules and have to be asked to leave. Jack peeked around the corner. Cal. That was all right.

Caleb Farnsworth had been his crew chief for more than two decades. Ten years Jack's senior, he'd been something of a father figure in the early days, but the relationship had evolved over time so they were more like brothers now. There wasn't much one didn't know about the other.

"Rough break," Cal said, as he entered the cramped lounge. He went to the refrigerator, got out a small can of tomato juice, pulled the soft silver tab off the opening and took a long sip.

"Barney all right?" Jack asked.

"Fine. His car's history, but the medics gave him a clean bill. A small abrasion on his cheek. Nothing that won't take care of itself in a few days."

"Good."

The pileup that resulted when Barney Constantine lost a wheel, slid up against the outside rail and bounced back into the pack behind him was nothing short of spectacular. He'd then been rammed by two other cars and bulldozed into the infield where he rolled four times before finally coming to a halt upside down. The media would no doubt be showing the video many times over the next few weeks and months. Fortunately the safety features built into NASCAR stock cars were such that it wasn't uncommon nowadays for drivers to walk away from even more scary crashes.

Cal sat on one of the gray vinyl-covered couches, threw an arm across the back and balanced one ankle on the other knee.

"You happen to look at the bottom of page three?"

Jack knew what he was referring to and had been expecting the question since he scanned the Greensboro newspaper in his motor home that morning over his first cup of coffee.

"I saw it." He took another long glug of his drink.

"You going?"

"No."

Cal didn't seem shocked by the answer or its terseness. "Why not?"

"Why should I? It's not like we were friends."

Cal examined the tomato juice can in his hand, took another sip and gazed up at this friend.

"She was the only wife you ever had, Jack. But she isn't really the point, is she? Funerals aren't for the dead. They're for the living, and the living in this case is your son, the son you haven't seen in twenty-five years."

"And whose fault is that?"

"A little late for the blame game, don't you think? Lillah's dead, Jack. It's a hackneyed phrase, but she can't hurt you anymore."

He was tempted to say she would never stop hurting him, but why bother? He'd lost that argument a quarter of a century ago when she left him, taking their son, *his son,* with her.

"The service is Tuesday."

Jack shrugged. The truth was he was sorry she was dead, not because he had any feelings for her, no positive ones, at least, but because even after all these years he still wanted her to tell him why. What had he done to make her toss him aside like so much road debris? What offense had he committed to warrant having his son torn from his life?

He also wondered if she would have told him she had no regrets, that she'd done the right thing. How could it have been right to take a child from his father, a father who loved and cherished him, then give him to another man?

But he knew it was all futile. Unless Lillah had changed dramatically over the past two and a half decades, which he seriously doubted, she wouldn't have given him a completely honest answer anyway.

In truth it had never been about the boy, never been about Jack. It had been about Lillah. Everything had always been about Lillah.

"I'll go with you, if you like," Cal offered, because he was a friend, and because he knew how painful it would be for Jack to face the son he hadn't seen since the boy was four years old.

"I said I'm not going." Jack tossed the empty plastic jug into the recycle bin and headed for the door.

HE ENTERED HIS MOTOR HOME and immediately began stripping off his smelly uniform. Yes, he'd seen the article. The paper was still sitting on the kitchen island folded with the notice centered. It wasn't long. It wasn't elaborate, just a formal statement that a funeral service would be conducted at Faith Chapel on the outskirts of Greensboro for Lillah Rendisi, née Neace, widow of the late European Formula 1 race car driver, Antonio Rendisi. Mrs. Rendisi, the article said, passed away two weeks ago at her villa outside Florence where she had been living for many years, but she had requested interment in the Neace family plot with her parents. It noted that she was survived by her son, Johnny Rendisi—but didn't mention Johnny's birth father was Jack Dolman, three-time NASCAR NEXTEL Cup Champion.

Depositing his soiled clothes in the hamper in his marble-tiled bathroom, Jack stepped into the shower and turned on all the jets. The initial blast of tepid water on his sweat-stained skin always felt like a reward after a race. He gradually raised the water temperature as he lathered up.

He'd met Lillah when they were both still in high school. He was racing street cars back then, souped-up jalopies that didn't look like much and had more exposed bondo than paint. Some of them were literally held together with baling wire. Their power trains frequently weren't much better. As for tires…they weren't really slicks; they were just bald.

Jack poured shampoo into his hair and massaged it in. Crazy days—and dangerous—but there was an excitement about them that couldn't be surpassed. Each driver had built his own car with money he'd begged, borrowed and worked his butt off for, sacking groceries or delivering newspapers, mowing lawns—whatever it took to buy a new part, a carburetor rebuilding kit or a new set of spark plugs. A driver knew his car, every flaw and quality it possessed, because he had built it himself, installed each of the parts, tuned it by sound and instinct, tested it on back roads and improvised dirt tracks.

When... *If* he won a race, he was as surprised as the people who stood by and cheered, and for the next week or until the next race, whichever came first, he was "The Champ."

Nobody kept scores or records. There were no write-ups in the local papers, no radio or TV interviews, no sponsors. There weren't any trophies, either, just the satisfaction of knowing he'd beat the other guys.

Lillah had gone to all the drag races, wearing her skimpy, tight halter tops and low-slung, clinging jeans. Every teenage male who saw her—and she was hard to miss—developed hormonal problems that plagued him for the rest of the day. Jack wasn't immune, but he already had a girl, a girl who happened to be Lillah's best friend. Then Margaret decided she liked dating a musician better than a race car driver, and Jack suddenly found himself free and brokenhearted. Lillah offered consolation. Well, what was a guy to do?

He was beginning to win more consistently by then and earning a reputation as a formidable contender. Word was spreading, as well, that he was on his way to the big time. Even before he graduated from high school, Charlie Hanks, who owned the biggest truck stop in the county, had offered to sponsor him in a couple of American Short Track Racing Associationsanctioned competitions. He didn't come in first, but he made a good enough showing that Charlie had been willing to stick by him. Eventually he won a few races, more doors began to open, and he was able to advance to the NASCAR Busch Series.

He wasn't an instant winner there, either, but he did all right. People with deeper pockets started bankrolling him. He still wasn't making a whole lot of money, but the prospect seemed closer that someday he could.

Then Lillah announced she was pregnant.

He was nineteen. So was she. Her mother prayed; her father got drunk. His parents insisted they were too young and too immature to be parents. They were right, of course, but as far as he was concerned, there was only one honorable thing to do. He married her.

The marriage was rocky from the start. She blamed him for the spot she was in—as if she'd had nothing to do with it. She complained about the ugliness and discomfort of being fat and pregnant. The pain of childbirth. The horror of having to change diapers. He saw only that he had a son.

If it hadn't been for Johnny, Jack would have asked for a divorce, but for Johnny's sake, Jack toughed it out. Things would settle down, he told himself, and for a while they seemed to. He was spending more time in Victory Lane, and Lillah was receiving more attention as the wife of a winner and the mother of his adorable child. Jack wasn't earning enough for them to live luxuriously yet, but their circumstances were improving.

The last thing Jack had expected was competition from another race car driver, and an open-wheel driver at that.

He and Lillah met Formula 1 champion, Antonio Rendisi, at Indianapolis. The Italian heartthrob was in the States on a tour, checking out America's version of Grand Prix racing. Lillah insisted on getting his autograph.

Standing amid a throng of mostly women admirers the tall, twenty-four-year-old bachelor gazed down at Lillah, took her hand and kissed it. He said *"bellissima"* and called her *"cara,"* then told her in his smooth, elegantly accented English she was one of the most beautiful women he had ever met. Lillah left, reluctantly, in a daze.

The three of them met again at Daytona the following week. What Jack didn't know was after that his wife kept meeting the Italian playboy privately when Jack was off preparing for races and trying to attract more and bigger sponsors. Four months later, his American tour complete, Rendisi returned to Italy. A month after that, while Jack was in Texas winning his third race in a row, Lillah and four-year-old Johnny were on an international flight to Rome.

Turning off the shower, Jack opened the stall door, grabbed a fluffy towel from the heated bar rack and dried himself off. Tomorrow he'd go to the gym and work out—hard. Maybe get Tony to give him a muscle-pounding massage to help relieve the tension.

He didn't hate Lillah anymore, he decided as he dressed, at least not to the depth he had back then. What was the point of hating the dead? But if she were alive he wouldn't go to see her, not after twenty-five years, so why attend her funeral service?

Except, dammit, Cal was right—his son would be

there. The son he had loved. The son he still loved. The son who, for all he knew, had completely forgotten him.

But how would Jack know if he didn't meet the boy—the man—now? And when he did, what would he say? "Hi, you probably don't remember me, but I'm your father."

CHAPTER TWO

"AMBER, FOR HEAVEN'S SAKE, will you please hurry up? This is a funeral, not a beauty pageant."

The bathroom door flew open and a young woman stepped out. Her long blond hair draped her shoulders like a silken veil. Green eye shadow subtly enhanced the greenish tint of her hazel eyes. Her lips were a shiny red. She was a knockout, and for a moment the sight of her made him forget why he'd been impatient with her.

He stepped over to her. "You're beautiful, *cara.*" He tried to put his arms around her.

"Oh, no you don't," she said, laughing, as she extended her arms, "or we'll never get out of here. Besides, you'll mess up my lipstick."

She was right. He remembered now why he'd been nagging her, but oh, the wait was worth it.

They rode the elevator down to the lobby where Amber's mother was waiting.

"I was just about to call up," Margaret said by way of greeting. She beheld the sight of her daughter and couldn't keep from smiling. Amber was wearing an Italian-designer knee-length black knit outfit with a modest string of small pearls and matching brooch for accent. She'd even pinned a delicate piece of Belgian black lace on her head, reminiscent of a mourner's mantilla.

"You look lovely, sweetheart," she told her daughter. The glow in Johnny's eyes testified that he totally agreed with her.

"I don't imagine they'll start without us," Amber observed, trying to sound casual, "but hadn't we better get going?"

Amber didn't like funerals, which she'd made clear that morning when she proposed not attending this one for Lillah. Margaret had argued that not going would be disrespectful to Johnny and his mother who had been so generous to her.

"It's almost over, *cara mia*," Johnny murmured, as he took her hands and tenderly kissed the tips of her fingers. "Thank you for being here with me. A man can do anything with a beautiful woman by his side."

What they had to do now was get through the next couple of hours. His mother's insistence on being brought back here for burial didn't make much sense to him. There was no family left. Her first husband, his father, was still around somewhere, but he hardly counted. His mother's parents were long dead. She had no brothers or sisters, and she'd lost track of what friends she might once have had in the area, with the exception of Margaret Truesdale, but Margaret was hardly justification for this ridiculous odyssey. His mom's place was in Italy, in the Rendisi family crypt with his stepfather, Antonio, the husband she'd lived with most of her life. But this was what she'd wanted, so Johnny was honoring it. That didn't mean he had to like it, though.

The funeral home had sent a limo, which was waiting under the portico of the luxury hotel's main entrance. The black-suited chauffeur opened the back door of the shiny Cadillac and stood by while the three of them got in. Silently the car glided into morning traffic.

"Thanks for handling the details," Johnny told Margaret. "I wouldn't have known where to start."

"Glad to help," she said. "Your mother became very special to me."

MARGARET GLANCED OVER at her daughter and marveled at how beautiful she truly was. At moments like these she seemed much older than her nineteen years. And that worried Margaret. Their year-long sojourn in Italy had brought a new level of maturity and refinement to her daughter, as Margaret had hoped it would, but ever since their return to the States Amber's behavior had become erratic, as if she couldn't decide if she wanted to be a polished European sophisticate or a rebellious American teenager.

Sure, the surroundings here were different. Their house in an older section of Greensboro was a far cry from the Rendisi villa outside Florence, and they didn't have servants at their beck and call the way they had there, but they weren't exactly poor. Margaret had suggested Amber enroll in college, since her education had been interrupted by their trip to Italy, but her daughter had rejected the notion out of hand. Margaret had no idea why. Amber had always enjoyed school. She'd been a good, enthusiastic student—at least until her senior year, but that hadn't been her fault.

Margaret sighed. Growing up seemed so much harder these days than it was when she was young.

"I don't know how much of a turnout there'll be at the church," she told Johnny. "The announcement of the service ran in the paper only once. I heard from a few old friends yesterday who said they'd try to be there, but I wouldn't count on a big crowd showing up."

"Her real friends were home in Italy," he replied. "I still don't understand why she wanted to be buried back here."

Margaret had a feeling she did and wondered if deep inside he might, too, and was not willing to admit it.

"She grew very nostalgic toward the end," Margaret said. "Maybe it was having me around. Getting to speak English regularly again probably put her in mind of a different time and place." With a self-deprecating snort, she added, "Or maybe it was my Southern drawl."

"There was nothing wrong with her Italian," Johnny commented.

Margaret had to smile. "No, there wasn't. When we were growing up I would never have imagined her even making an attempt to learn a foreign language, much less speaking one well. We had to take two years of French in high school, and she was terrible at it."

Johnny emitted a soft chuckle. "It never got any better. On the few occasions when she attempted to speak French with our guests, it would have been embarrassing if she hadn't been so willing to joke about it."

Another change in Lillah. Margaret had no recollection of her being able to laugh at herself.

"Dad spoke excellent French," Johnny went on. "He

could never understand how Mom could learn one language and not another."

They turned onto a secondary road, passed a few scattered clapboard homes huddled meekly under towering maple and oak trees. Most of the houses had been there when Margaret and Lillah were growing up and hadn't changed much. A few were newer, bigger, but were still not the kind that left a lasting impression.

"That's where your mom grew up." Margaret pointed to a shake-shingle house that appeared to need a fresh coat of paint as much today as it had thirty years ago. "I lived down the road a ways, but our place is gone now."

"Doesn't look like much," he said.

She shook her head. "It wasn't." She could see an addition at the rear of the bungalow. "Just four rooms back then."

"What were they like?" he asked. "My mother's parents?"

"You don't remember them at all?"

He shook his head. "Never saw them once we went to Italy, and I don't recall much before that."

Like your father or how much he loved you.

"Ordinary people, really. Your grandfather worked in a hardware store. Never missed a day's work, as far as I know."

"And my grandmother?" Johnny asked.

"I guess you'd call Ida Mae a country woman. She didn't get involved outside the home very much, except for church and her quilting circle. She did wonderful needlework. Died of cancer a year or two after Lillah went to Italy. Your grandfather was killed in a traffic accident a few years later."

Lillah hadn't come home from Italy for either funeral, Margaret reflected but didn't say anything.

They arrived at a small whitewashed country church, set back on a lush green lawn. It had been outside Greensboro city limits when Margaret and Lillah were growing up. Now it was incorporated and surrounded by an upscale housing development.

The hearse was already parked on the narrow asphalt road behind the building at the edge of the cemetery, the casket suspended over an open grave a short distance away.

A cluster of people was standing around talking among themselves. They turned almost as one when the limo came to a halt at the end of the footpath leading to the burial site. The chauffeur opened the vehicle's back door. Johnny stepped out first, offered his hand to Amber, then her mother.

Nervously, Margaret studied the waiting mourners and recognized familiar faces. She couldn't be sure if she was relieved or disappointed to find Jack Dolman wasn't among them.

The next ten minutes were taken up with introductions and greetings. For Margaret it felt good to be among friends she hadn't seen in over a year. They hugged her and kissed her cheek. The women patted Amber's hands and told her how beautiful she was.

The person of real interest, of course, was Johnny. The men, all of them older, were guarded, not quite sure what to make of this tall, handsome gentleman who was now as much a stranger in the land of his birth

as any of them would have been in the heart of Rome
or Florence. The women were captivated by the way he
held their hands when they were introduced and by the
slightly foreign lilt of his speech that echoed more of
Britain than North Carolina. Dora Sue Luckett, who'd
gone to school with Margaret and Lillah, gazed up at
him like a lovesick adolescent and said, "You have your
father's beautiful blue eyes."

Margaret cringed. From the many photographs of
Antonio Rendisi she'd seen scattered around the villa, she
knew he had brown eyes. Fortunately just then, the
minister chose to make his appearance. He was wearing
a flowing cream-colored vestment and a long purple stole
trimmed in gold. Not more than forty, he couldn't possibly
have known Lillah or her son. He'd almost reached them
when Margaret heard a car door slam. She looked toward
the curb and felt a sudden weakness in her knees.

Jack Dolman, wearing a dark blue pin-striped suit,
white shirt and plain navy-blue tie, was approaching the
assembled crowd.

Margaret studied his somber face. She'd seen his
image in newspapers and magazines over the years, and
occasionally on TV, but this was the first time she'd seen
him in the flesh in almost three decades.

Remarkably the years didn't seem to have changed
him. He was still tall, of course, and lean. His features
had hardened a bit with age but not in an unpleasant
way. He was more mature now than he had been back
then, but she could still glimpse the handsome teenager.
What was missing was the twinkle in his eyes.

Because she had been so focused on Jack, she hadn't

witnessed the transformation in Johnny, but a murmur, a shuffling of feet, made her turn her head.

His suntanned face had darkened, the beautiful blue eyes Dora Sue had commented on had hardened and narrowed. He stepped forward.

"What the hell are you doing here?" he demanded, his voice deep, clipped, challenging.

"I came to pay my respects," Jack said, after a slight pause, without matching the other man's confrontational attitude.

"You have no right to be here. I want you to leave. Now."

JACK STUDIED the young man standing before him. The pictures he'd seen of him in magazines hadn't done him justice. They captured his good looks well enough but not the fire, not the virility that emanated from him. The flood of pride Jack felt took him by surprise.

"She was my wife, son."

"You have no right to call me that. I'm not your son, and she ceased being your wife a long time ago. I asked you to leave. You're not welcome here."

Jack had been waiting twenty-five years for this moment, when he could once again gaze into the face of his son, the boy he had cradled in his arms. He beheld the man now and felt deep sadness for all the intervening years since last they had been together. So much time lost, so many dreams and opportunities unrealized, never to be retrieved. Gone forever.

Why? What had he done to be so punished, except make love with the wrong woman?

Jack continued to study his son, then walked past him to the graveside and placed the red rose he'd been holding in his right hand on the lid of the casket. He spread his palm on the polished wood for a second, then turned to leave. But before he did he faced his boy. "I am your father. I have always been your father, and I always will be."

Johnny's jaw tightened. He glowered, lips tight, hands clenched.

Jack swallowed the lump that had suddenly formed in his throat. The pride he'd felt tasted like ashes in his mouth now for having failed to be a father to his son. Their reunion shouldn't be like this, but he was powerless to change it—just as he had been impotent to alter the course of events twenty-five years ago.

He surveyed the crowd in the background, recognized Margaret—sweet Megs—nodded, turned on his heel and retraced his steps.

CHAPTER THREE

"JACK, WAIT."

Margaret's familiar voice. Even after all these years it conjured up a warm feeling. He was tempted to keep going.

He stopped, paused and turned just as she caught up with him.

"Jack, I'm sorry." She stood in front of him, concern etching the corners of her light-brown hazel eyes. He could see she wanted to say more, but for the moment they just stood there, taking each other in.

He should say something, but he didn't know what. It was nice seeing her, but this was no time for silly platitudes, even if the sentiment was true.

"He doesn't understand," Margaret finally said.

"He's not alone." Jack had anticipated reserve, uneasiness, maybe even hostility after so many years, but not the kind of venom he'd just encountered. "You better get back. They're waiting for you."

The group behind her was staring at them in silence. Johnny's arms were folded, his dark features a stone mask of rage.

"I shouldn't have come."

"You have every right to be here," she said.

"Go on back." He started to turn away.

"Tomorrow," she blurted out, almost breathless. "Can we get together tomorrow? I...I was with her at the end, Jack. There's a lot we have to talk about, a lot of catching up to do."

"Why?" He didn't mean it to sound like a challenge, as though the invitation was onerous.

"Please, Jack." A pause. "How about we meet at the Arboretum at three."

He caught himself smiling. He hadn't been to the Arboretum in years. He and Margaret used to stroll there when they were going together back in another life.

"You sure?"

She nodded.

He took a deep breath. "I'm not convinced it's a good idea, but okay. At three."

He turned away again and this time continued on to his car. He glanced over the roof of his maroon Mustang as he was getting in and saw Margaret being received with confused expressions on the faces of the mourners. She didn't look back.

THE SERVICE was predictable, appropriate for the occasion and, Margaret reflected, should have elicited tears, but it hadn't, maybe because her thoughts hadn't been on the woman in the casket but on Lillah's ex-husband.

As for Johnny, any tears he might have shed had all been in private. He'd been stoic, too, at the elaborate religious service in the centuries-old church on the outskirts of Florence. Only the servants who had attended the ancient ritual had displayed any emotion.

"That son of a bitch had no right showing up here today. What did he come for? To gloat?" Johnny was sitting between the two women in the back of the limousine. Margaret could feel the negative vibes radiating off him. "Did you know he was coming?"

Margaret shook her head. "No."

Yet she'd been hoping he would show up. He looked good. In spite of the hurt expression in his eyes. Jack looked good.

"So you didn't arrange it?"

She felt her hands get clammy and unexpected tears begin to well. On the way here Johnny had thanked her for her help. Now he was attacking her as if she were the enemy.

"No, I didn't arrange it." She turned away from him and stared out the window as they drove by the dilapidated house his mother had grown up in.

"He probably saw the notice in the paper like everybody else," Amber contributed. "You heard what he said. He came to pay his respects. He is, after all, your daddy."

Johnny glared at her. "Don't ever call him that. He may be my father in the biological sense, but that's all. My name is Rendisi, not Dolman."

"Well, excuse me," Amber snapped back. "You don't have to take my head off."

"I'm sorry his appearance upset you," Margaret muttered a minute later, still facing the window. "He's really not a bad man."

"You don't know anything about it," Johnny insisted, "so let's drop it, shall we?"

She was tempted to tell him she probably knew more about it than he did, but there was no point in antagonizing him.

"Fine," she said, and resumed her silence.

LATER THAT AFTERNOON Vaughn Steiner, two-time NASCAR NEXTEL Cup Champion and now owner of Steiner Racing, watched the shiny black Lamborghini pull into his driveway and the driver extricate himself from it. Rendisi was tall, square-shouldered, dark-haired and impressively built. He'd called unexpectedly two hours earlier requesting an appointment at Steiner's earliest convenience. For anyone else, the team owner would have put the meeting off until the next day, maybe later, but the sense of urgency the European Grand Prix driver had quietly conveyed, combined with Steiner's own curiosity, was enough to prompt him to rearrange his schedule.

"Thank you for agreeing to see me on such short notice," Rendisi said, as he approached the opened front door and accepted his host's outstretched hand.

Steiner led him into the sun-filled living room. They were alone in the house. His wife, Gabby, was out shopping for baby clothes with her mother and wouldn't be home for hours, his seven-year-old daughter Stephanie was in school, and the housekeeper had left at noon.

"First, let me express my condolences on the loss of your mother," Steiner said. "I read about it in the paper. I had no idea she was American, much less from here."

"Thank you," Rendisi replied but didn't comment further.

Steiner motioned him to the couch. "May I get you something to drink? Coffee? Iced tea? Something stronger perhaps."

At his guest's polite refusal, Steiner took an easy chair on the other side of the coffee table. The two men sat facing each other.

"I must admit I was surprised to receive your call, Mr. Rendisi. What can I do for you?"

Rendisi planted his feet squarely on the floor, placed one elbow on the armrest of the sofa and propped the other on the cushion beside him. "I want to race in the NEXTEL Cup Series, Mr. Steiner, and I'd like to do so as a member of your team."

Steiner raised an eyebrow and studied him. It was an interesting idea. The question that came immediately to mind, though, was why. "You're a Formula 1 World champion. Why NASCAR?"

His dark-haired visitor tilted his head to the side but maintained firm eye contact, the hint of a smile on his lips. "The challenge."

Steiner grinned. He suspected there was more to it than that. Crossover between the two forms of auto racing wasn't unheard of, but it was rare.

"You're bored with Grand Prix racing?" he asked.

There was a momentary flicker in Rendisi's blue eyes before he chuckled. "Not at all, but I've become fascinated with NASCAR, especially the NEXTEL Series."

Steiner was tempted to press for more information. If the man was really searching for variety, why not explore the NASCAR Craftsman Truck Series, or drag racing, for that matter. But he let the matter rest for the time being. The other man's motives probably weren't germane. The pertinent question was whether he could be successful at it.

"About the only things the two types of racing have in common," Steiner noted, "is that the cars have four rubber tires." Though the tires themselves were very different. Even the steering wheels weren't the same. In NASCAR they were utilitarian and detachable. In Formula 1 they served as high-tech control panels. "The tracks don't resemble each other—" primarily oval versus roads courses "—and the rules have very little in common."

"Exactly. That's what I find so appealing. Stock car and open-wheel racing are miles apart."

"I would have thought if you wanted to conquer the American scene, you'd go for Indy."

The other man shrugged dismissively. "I don't think Indy racing would be much of a challenge."

Steiner threw back his head and laughed. "I promise not to tell them you said that."

Rendisi remained serious. "I want a greater challenge, Mr. Steiner, something that'll fully test my skills."

"You think you can master this alien environment?"

Rendisi nodded. "I'm hoping you'll afford me the opportunity to find out."

Steiner continued to study him. He didn't doubt the truth of what he was hearing, he just didn't believe he was hearing it all. He had himself entertained notions of driving in Grand Prix a long time ago, but he'd never considered giving up NASCAR to do it. Racing was in his blood, and NASCAR was his blood type. Rendisi, it would seem, was less parochial.

"There are a lot of NASCAR teams," he said. "I'm certainly flattered that you've come to me, but I have to ask again. Why? Why Steiner Racing?"

"I've studied you, Mr. Steiner. I know you were a driver, that you won the Cup twice. You're intimately familiar with NASCAR from the inside out, not just from an owner's perspective. I admire that. I'm also aware that you're willing to take chances on people. Last year you had the only female driver in the NEXTEL Series, a rookie. She didn't just place or do well. She won the Cup. I don't believe that was an accident or simply a matter of good fortune."

Calculated flattery? Perhaps. Rendisi struck Steiner as a man who was good with words.

"If you examine *my* record," Rendisi went on, "you'll learn I'm a strong competitor, too. I drive to win, not just to go fast. My decision to come into NASCAR isn't a whim, Mr. Steiner. I want to win. I want to win very badly, and I think you can help me achieve that goal. Will you?"

Steiner sat back and considered the proposition carefully. With the Rendisi name and reputation, finding a sponsor shouldn't be difficult. Whether he did well or poorly, Steiner would be credited with being willing to take a chance.

"I like a challenge, too, Mr. Rendisi, so let's see if you're cut out for stock car racing."

He rose to his feet. His guest did the same.

"Come to Charlotte next Monday." He furnished specific directions on how to get to the track there and

who to ask for. "We'll be test-driving a car we just
finished rebuilding. Let's see what you've got. If you
don't get dizzy going around in circles," he added light-
heartedly, "and you're still interested in pursuing the
NASCAR NEXTEL challenge, we'll go from there."

CHAPTER FOUR

ON WEDNESDAY AFTERNOON Jack arrived at the Arboretum early for his appointment with Margaret, parked in the lot outside the entrance gates, sat in the car for several minutes, then got out and began nervously pacing.

If he were a drinking man he'd probably be well fortified by now, but he hadn't consumed more than an occasional beer or glass of wine in years. Even now he wasn't tempted by alcohol, but he did miss the promise of escape it offered, a promise, which for him, it had never fulfilled.

He'd been trying to recall the last time he'd seen Margaret Cooper. Truesdale now. It must have been after he and Lillah were married, right after Johnny was born. A casual meeting. In a supermarket? A drugstore? They'd exchanged pleasantries but avoided eye contact, each eager to move on.

He hadn't expected to see her at the cemetery yesterday, though on reflection he realized he should have. The notice in the paper. She would have seen it and wanted to pay her respects. Even when he and Margaret had broken up she'd been gracious and tactful. She'd met somebody else, she said. It wasn't Jack's fault, nothing he'd done or hadn't done. She hoped he'd understand.

He hadn't.

But the news that she'd been with Lillah at the end… He hadn't anticipated that.

She still looked good. The years hadn't been unkind. She'd been pretty as a teenager. She was still pretty, but more complex now, more mature and sophisticated, which made her even more intriguing.

He'd cared deeply for Margaret, loved her and thought she loved him. But what do high school kids know about love? They'd both been too young to understand much beyond the physical and emotional attraction, an attraction she'd never let him take all the way. Given time, though, Jack was sure their relationship would have matured into genuine love and affection. Obviously, she hadn't been willing to wait. Had be been too slow? He must have, because Gary Truesdale came along, and she ran away from Jack as fast as she could.

On the rebound he'd let himself be enticed by her best friend, Lillah Neace, more out of spite than affinity, and because Lillah had been willing, even eager, to satisfy his needs in the way Margaret had not been. Yeah, he'd really hit the jackpot with Lillah. Too bad he hadn't been smart enough to protect himself—and her.

He heard the crunch of tires on the gravel behind him and turned. Margaret was right on time. She'd always been punctual.

She climbed out of her three-year-old blue Ford Escort and clicked the door locks. Jack noticed immediately that instead of a stylish outfit like the one she'd had on yesterday, she was wearing stone-washed jeans and a bulky red sweater, walking shoes rather than heeled pumps. Her auburn hair, darker than he remembered it from their youth, was no longer piled high on her head but gathered loosely in back and tied with a red ribbon at the nape of her neck. Casual, unpretentious, yet on Margaret it was classy, elegant.

"Thank you for coming," she said, as she walked toward him.

"Thanks for asking me."

She smiled at him, polite amusement dancing in her hazel-brown eyes. "But you're really not sure you want to be here, are you?"

He clutched both her hands with his. They felt warm, soft, gentle. "I know I'm glad to see you again."

And he was. He'd thought a lot about her last night, more than he'd thought about any woman in longer than he could remember.

They walked side by side toward the main entrance to the Arboretum.

"It was foolish of me to show up yesterday," he said.

"I wondered if you would and was disappointed when I arrived and didn't see you there. I'm sorry about what happened."

"In his place, after all the lies Lillah probably told him about me—" he lifted his shoulders in a lazy shrug "—it was crazy of me to expect otherwise."

They entered the park.

"I had no idea you'd kept in contact with her," he said as they passed a large map display of the layout of the grounds.

It was the end of November. Most of the deciduous trees had lost their leaves, though a few still greedily hung on to their colorful autumn foliage.

"Actually, until last year, I hadn't," she said, "not beyond Christmas cards. Then, late last summer, I received a letter from her. Antonio had died the year before, and she'd just been diagnosed with inoperable cancer. Her doctors had given her less than a year to live. She asked if I would come over and spend some time with her. I'd gone back to nursing full-time after Gary died. Lillah offered to pay all my expenses, plus a salary, if I'd stay with her. She invited my daughter, Amber, to be her houseguest, as well."

They started down a gravel path, the small gray stones crunching softly under their feet.

"Lillah was lonely, Jack. Her husband was dead. Her son spent most of his time traveling all over the world racing Formula 1 cars. She had plenty of friends and acquaintances in her social circle, but as she saw the end approaching she wanted something they couldn't give her. Contact with her roots, I guess."

"So you became her nurse."

Margaret shook her head. "I had no medical standing over there, and from everything I observed she was receiving excellent care. At first I was sort of a paid companion, but over time we became friends again. Confidantes."

"You said yesterday you were with her when she died." He pictured the Lillah he'd known so many years ago, propped up dramatically in a brocade-covered canopy bed in a dark-paneled chamber, watery light streaming in through leaded-glass windows. "Did she suffer?"

"Her caregivers made sure she didn't. The end was peaceful, Jack. No pain, just a quiet retreat into eternal sleep."

"Nobody can ask for more."

They continued to stroll along the path in silence for several minutes. Small signs identified the various trees, but they ignored them.

He started to reach for her hand but caught himself in time. The gesture would have been too intimate, and he was sure she wouldn't welcome it. She'd left him for somebody else, after all.

"You haven't asked if she talked about you," Margaret finally commented.

He would have liked to say it didn't matter, that it had all been over between them ages ago, that he never gave her a thought anymore. But it would have been a lie. At some level he'd never stopped thinking about Lillah, about Johnny. When he won a race, he wished he had them to share the euphoria with. When he did poorly he longed for the kind of comfort only a family could provide. How many times had he imagined his little boy gazing up at him and calling him Daddy, and saying he was proud of him, or telling him the loss didn't matter, that there would be another race.

"Did she?" he asked.

"I know it's probably small consolation now, Jack, but she told me she very much regretted what she'd done to you."

He took a deep breath. Did hearing that help?

"You're right." He wondered why his heart was suddenly beating harder. "It is small consolation."

He looked straight ahead as they continued their aimless journey.

"I forgave her for leaving me a long time ago." At least he liked to think he had. What he hadn't forgiven was her taking his son away from him.

"Our marriage was a mistake from the start. Nowadays a situation like ours would be handled very differently. No shotgun weddings anymore, not that her father ever threatened me, but I felt obligated."

"Because of Johnny."

"He's my son, Megs."

She stopped and smiled at him. "Megs," she repeated. "No one's called me that in years."

They resumed walking.

"I heard about Gary's death a few years ago," he said moments later. "I'm sorry. I would have sent flowers, but the news was a couple of months old when I got it."

"That's all right," she said. "It would have been nice hearing from you, though."

THEY'D BEEN SWEETHEARTS for more than two years when she finally allowed herself to be distracted by Gary Truesdale, the trumpeter in a jazz band. He'd been gregarious, fun-loving and talented with a horn, and he hung out with people who had clean hands and were fascinating mavericks. Something unexpected was always going on in Gary's world. With Jack it seemed all he and his friends ever talked about was cars and racing. Oh, she enjoyed the races, the excitement of the crowds, the noise of the cars, but afterward…it seemed so boring to her most of the time. What did she care about compression ratios, timing adjustments and points settings? A lot of it she didn't understand or couldn't get enthusiastic about when it was explained to her.

But Gary and his bunch…they were different, more eclectic in their interests. Music was important, but so were politics and art and current events. With Jack she always knew where they would be, who they'd be with, and what they would be doing on Friday and Saturday night. With Gary she never did. A gig somewhere, sure, but afterward they'd go to a different nightclub or to a play, or maybe sit around a coffeehouse gossiping or arguing politics. Gary didn't have any more money than Jack, but somehow he made it feel better spent.

But was it love?

"Were you happy?" Jack asked.

How could she tell him she never felt about Gary the way she'd felt about him, that for the twenty years of their marriage she stifled the guilt of secretly comparing her husband to the man she'd let go. Maybe that was why their marriage never became the idyllic happily-ever-after relationship she'd dreamed of. She'd tried to console herself with the bromide that it probably wouldn't have been any better with Jack, but she never quite succeeded in convincing herself it was true. For one thing, she was sure Jack would never have been unfaithful to her the way Gary had been.

"It wasn't perfect," she admitted now, "but we kept working at it." At least she liked to think *she* had. But marriage involved two people and when only one was trying, it was doomed to failure. "You never remarried, did you?"

He shook his head. "After y—" He was going to say *you,* she realized, which added to her sense of guilt for having failed them both. At the same time that slip of the tongue made her feel incredibly special. "After Lillah," he corrected himself, "I wasn't in a marrying frame of mind."

"Didn't trust women?" she teased.

He snorted. "More like didn't trust my judgment about them. My record isn't very good. The only two women in my life walked out on me."

She felt the rebuke, though she doubted he'd intended the comment as one. Remembering the kind of man he had been she reckoned he'd probably blamed himself for their breakup.

They reached the gazebo. Jack took out a handkerchief and brushed off a section of the bench lining its perimeter. She sat, and he settled beside her, within reach but not touching.

"Tell me about her." He stretched out his long legs. "Tell me about Lillah."

CHAPTER FIVE

MARGARET WAS SURE she heard affection in his request. Jack had every reason to despise his former wife, and Margaret supposed at some point he probably had. But love and hate can be so tightly wrapped around each other. As much as Lillah had hurt him, Margaret doubted Jack had ever wanted to hurt her back. He wasn't at heart a vindictive person, and it wasn't in his nature to cling to negative emotions. Pessimists didn't consistently win, and he had—at least in the world of racing.

"Lillah still had the laugh," Margaret replied. "Remember how she could captivate a room full of people with her laugh. She held on to it till the end, a cigarette and whiskey laugh by then, husky and worldly, but it still had that something that made people turn their heads and involuntarily grin with her."

Margaret gazed down at her hands, crossed them in her lap.

"She had a good life, Jack, at least in the material sense. The big apartment in the heart of Rome. The villa in the Tuscan hills outside Florence. Servants, cars, the use of a private plane. Plenty of time and money for shopping sprees. Wealth, prestige and always people around her."

"She never did like being alone," he commented.

"But at heart she was. Proves the old adages, I guess, that money can't buy happiness, and you can be lonely in the midst of a crowd."

He rose to his feet and paced the confines of the pretty cage. "So what went wrong? Why wasn't she happy?"

Margaret closed her eyes for a moment. "Antonio wasn't the best husband in the world. Not physically abusive. Lillah admitted he had never struck her or threatened to, even when they were shouting at each other at the top of their lungs. Most of the time he was polite, even charming, and always generous. He just wasn't faithful, and he didn't even bother trying to hide his indiscretions. He kept a mistress. Two of them at one point. Didn't care that Lillah knew about them, either. She could have invited them over for an afternoon aperitif or gone boutique shopping with them, and he wouldn't have been in the least upset or embarrassed."

"She had Johnny. She had my son."

Not *her* son, or *their* son. *His* son.

"Did you know Antonio couldn't have kids?"

He stared at her for a second. "No. But then I can't say I ever gave it any thought. I assumed they didn't have any more children because they didn't want to."

"Lillah told me she'd hoped, expected to have a slew of them. It was one of her greatest disappointments that there weren't *molto bambini* running through the house, especially daughters to spoil and buy fancy clothes for. She liked being a mom—"

"At least after the diaper stage."

"But it wasn't until after she'd left you and married Antonio that she found out he was sterile. Some child-hood fever or other. She was furious when he finally told her. She accused him of marrying her under false pre-tenses. He laughed and reminded her he'd never promised her more kids. Which she had to admit was true. He'd talked about Johnny all the time, promised to be a good papa to him, but on reflection she realized he'd never mentioned giving him little brothers and sisters to play with."

"She wanted to get pregnant again with me," Jack muttered. "When I reminded her how much she hated being pregnant, she just laughed it aside and said she knew what to expect now. I told her we had to wait until I was better established. It wasn't that I didn't want more kids. I did, but at that point in my career, and the way she was spending money, I didn't see how we could afford another mouth to feed. Not then, at least." He shook his head. "Maybe if I'd understood how serious she was... Damn."

"She threatened to leave Antonio and come back to you, because you'd give her more children."

His head shot up. "Are you serious?"

"That's what she told me."

"You believed her?"

"By then she had no reason to lie, not to me, Jack."

"Why didn't she contact me? Together we could have—"

"Antonio told her she was free to leave anytime she wanted, but she would do so without Johnny. He'd formally adopted the boy by then, given him his name. Under Italian law, that made Johnny his son, his legal heir, and Antonio had enough money to pay lawyers and buy judges to make sure Johnny stayed with him."

"Bastard." Jack paced back and forth, hands in his pockets, as if he didn't dare let them loose. "So she stayed with him. Was it for Johnny, or was it for the money?"

"She liked the money," Margaret said. "No question about that, but by then you were starting to make a name for yourself in NASCAR, and she'd been around auto racing long enough to know there was money in it. No, I don't think she stayed for the wealth or the prestige. She stayed for Johnny. Not that it did her much good."

"What do you mean?"

"Antonio eventually stole him away from her."

"I don't understand. How?"

"How do you think? Racing."

Jack closed his eyes and sighed. He had himself taken the four-year-old out to his first go-kart track and taught him how to drive. It was what racing people did. Boys needed fathers, and what better way to bond with your son than by doing things together, having common interests? Jack had never thought of it as a way of stealing the boy from his mother, though. Had Antonio done it intentionally?

"As I'm sure you already know," Margaret continued, "by the time Johnny was sixteen he was competing all over the continent. Lillah attended most of his European races, even went to a few in the Far East, proudly stood with him on the podium when he received his medals and awards, but after the champagne, the interviews and photo shoots were over, Johnny retired with his father to the manly world of Formula 1 racing, where mamas had no place."

"I'll grant him this," Jack said with grudging respect, "Antonio seems to have taught him well. Johnny's one of the top Formula 1 drivers in the world."

"A chip off the old block all right." She saw Jack frown. "I'm not referring to Antonio but to you," she hastened to clarify. "He reminds me of you in so many ways. He's more of an extrovert than you were, but he's capable of the same single-minded determination you always had, and apparently still have, based on where you are today. But there's a lot of his mother in him, too. He can be headstrong, vain and selfish while at the same time being capable of tremendous generosity. I guess he gets that from both of you."

"And what did he get from Antonio?" Jack asked.

"The playboy syndrome. Johnny has quite a reputation with the ladies." She paused. "My daughter fell instantly under his spell."

"Was she the one in the black dress, standing next to him?"

Margaret nodded.

"She's beautiful."

Margaret was surprised he'd noticed. His visit to the churchyard had been so brief and his attention had naturally been on his son. Except that Amber was tall, blond, willowy and striking. In comparable circumstances, would a woman have noticed a particularly handsome man, someone like Johnny, for example, among a small group of mourners? Probably.

"Thank you, but she's only nineteen."

"Nineteen? I would have said she was older."

"At thirteen she could have passed for twenty-three. Used to scare the daylights out of her father. Gary kept threatening to buy a shotgun."

Jack laughed. "I would, too." Then he grew serious. "Ten years isn't a big deal between thirty and forty or forty and fifty, but it is between nineteen and twenty-nine. Does he usually go for teenagers?"

"Not according to Lillah. When Amber and I first got over there, he treated her like a sister, seemed to enjoy her company, took her places. But as you say, she's a beautiful girl. Of legal age. And he's a virile man who appreciates the opposite sex. I guess it was inevitable that their relationship would progress to something more intimate."

"Have you talked to her about this?"

"Of course, I have," she replied. "She's my daughter. She says she loves him, and she's convinced he loves her."

"And what does he say?"

"That he cares very deeply for her. He hasn't used the *L* word, but he assures me he would never do anything to hurt her."

"You believe him?"

"I believe he means what he says—"

"But that his actions may not conform to his words."

"At heart he wants to do the right thing, but so many of us hurt other people without thinking, without intending to."

Jack gazed at her for a moment, as though he were unsure how to respond or even if he should try. Did he realize she was trying to apologize for walking out on him so long ago?

He turned around and spread his hands on the gazebo's decorative rail. She wondered what was going through his mind.

"Another thing Johnny learned from Antonio—" Margaret went on a minute later.

Jack turned to face her.

"—is a strong competitive instinct." She hesitated. "There's something you need to know, Jack. Johnny went to see Vaughn Steiner yesterday afternoon. He made the appointment as soon as we got back from the cemetery. He's scheduled to go to Charlotte Monday to do a test drive."

Jack stared at her, his jaw slack, then he threw back his head and laughed. "He's planning to race in NASCAR against me? Well, well."

MONDAY WAS BRIGHT and clear, the air cool and crisp, December chilly but not raw cold. Vaughn Steiner stood at the wall and clicked the stopwatch he held in his right hand as the Number 581 car screamed by. "Wow, 44.6."

"I got 44.8," Mac Roberts, his senior crew chief, said, holding out his own micrometer.

"I won't quibble," Steiner replied. "He's running better than 200 miles an hour."

"By himself," Roberts pointed out.

Steiner nodded. Running fast on a clear track was no great achievement for an experienced race car driver. Of course, in this setting Rendisi didn't exactly fit that description. Not only was this track unfamiliar, the vehicle itself was unlike any he'd ever driven professionally. Even the vocabulary they used in NASCAR was different from what he was accustomed to in the world of Grand Prix racing. Mac's title, for example, was crew chief, not racing engineer, though the functions of the two were essentially the same.

"Let's give him some competition and see how he does," Steiner said.

Roberts spoke into his handheld radio. Five seconds later two stock cars rumbled down the alley between the rows of garages. They turned left onto the track and shattered the air as their engines screamed and accelerated.

Steiner announced into the mic of his headset. "Company's arrived."

Rendisi zoomed by on the inside. Behind him the other two cars, unnumbered, one black, the other red, tooled along at the top of the steeply banked track. As soon as Rendisi passed below them, they dropped down. The red one slipped in directly behind him, the black crowded him on the right. Rendisi was still on the inside, in the command position, as he cruised along at track speed, about 180 miles per hour.

"Now," Steiner said into his mic.

The driver of the red car slipped out from behind Rendisi, moved to the right, got on the tail of the black car and drafted him. Together the two interlopers built up speed and inched ahead on the outside of the Number 581 car.

They approached Turn One. Entering it, Rendisi instinctively eased off slightly on the gas. The black and red cars shot ahead of him on the outside of the curve.

Within three seconds they were in the left lane in front of him. Rendisi had gone from first to third.

"That ought to take some of the lead out of his pencil," Roberts said with a snicker.

"Let's see what he does now," Steiner replied. "Open it up," he instructed the lead drivers.

Before the black and red cars could slip to the right to give Rendisi access to the inside lane, however, the Formula 1 driver had already shot up to the right of the lead car. He crowded it, forcing the driver more and more to the left. He would have to either pull out in front of him, if he had the power, or back off, rather than violate the inside line. The red car would also be in jeopardy of disqualifying himself if he attempted a draft at this point. He dropped back. When the black car reluctantly eased off, as well, Rendisi stomped on the accelerator and shot ahead on the straightaway.

A good move under the circumstances, since his sparring partners weren't anxious to mangle their vehicles. In an actual race, however, chassis cosmetics didn't weigh heavily in a decision. Replacing damaged body panels was routine, so the inside driver would have no qualms about sideswiping the car trying to box him in.

The other problem with Rendisi's current maneuver was that he was coming into Turn Three too fast.

Roberts muttered a cussword. It seemed almost certain the nice shiny restored car was about to rejoin history.

The red and black cars obviously saw disaster ahead, too, because they both hit their brakes hard enough to give Rendisi space, uncertain if the novice driver would choose the long, high-banked outside route to escape his predicament or continue to hold the middle ground.

Rendisi did neither.

While his pursuers lagged far behind he stayed in the middle and jammed his brakes just as he was about to enter the turn, bringing his speed down enough to claim the inside of the curve.

"Slick," Roberts muttered with grudging respect.

"There are only three cars on the track," Steiner pointed out. "Pull that stunt with forty others out there and we could have had a forty-two car pileup."

Roberts chuckled. "And a winner."

"Do it again," Steiner instructed the team cars through his mic.

This time the black car pulled up on the Number 581 car's right side, the red falling in closely behind him. Again they formed a draft and once more started to pull ahead of Rendisi.

Anticipating a repetition of the earlier maneuver, Rendisi changed tactics. As they approached Turn One, he pushed them farther to the right, higher up the steep bank toward the wall. Then, between Turns One and Two, he cut sharply to the left, again dropped down to the inside of the track and was instantly ahead of his companions.

"No pileup that time." Roberts grinned with satisfaction. "He's a quick study."

"Or blessed with beginner's luck, which seems more likely. With only three cars out there. Rendisi's good," Steiner conceded, "but I guarantee he's not nearly as good as he thinks he is. He seems to have the potential, though."

"Sounds like you've made a decision." Roberts rubbed his chin. "You sure you want to take on an open-wheel driver, boss? Aside from being cocky—or maybe because they are—they tend to have a hard time making the transition. Not many have succeeded. And this guy's got winner's trophies to prove how smart he is. Prima donnas can be awfully disruptive."

Steiner didn't dispute the point, because he knew it was true. This guy had come to him from his mother's funeral. Why? Had she elicited some promise from him? Seemed like a stretch. Rendisi was holding something back.

"That's why we're going to work him hard over the next couple of months. To see if he has what it takes."

CHAPTER SIX

THERE WAS NO DIRECT contact between Jack and his son in the weeks following Lillah's funeral, not that the famous European Formula 1 race car driver hadn't been in the public's eye. Every couple of days brought another story in the news, another magazine article about the handsome Grand Prix driver signing on with Steiner Racing to compete in the upcoming season for the NASCAR NEXTEL Series Cup. He was constantly giving TV interviews.

He spoke freely and enthusiastically about the man he called his father, the late, famous Antonio Rendisi, and the invaluable inspiration and training he'd received under his tutelage. Never once was there any mention of his having been adopted by the wealthy Italian.

"Don't tell me not to take it personally," Jack told Margaret. They were in a quiet restaurant in Greensboro, their second dinner since his disastrous meeting with his son at the cemetery. "That's precisely what it is—personal. Why does he hate me so much?"

Jack had specifically requested a corner booth, where they were less likely to be seen by autograph seekers. Last time he'd made the mistake of taking her to a more

popular, open floorplan eatery, and they'd been interrupted so often they'd hardly gotten to taste their food,
at least not while it was hot.

Margaret had been absolutely gracious about it,
though, smiled at the people who invaded their privacy,
exchanged pleasantries with them. Jack found being with
her so natural, as if the intervening years hadn't existed.

"I never met Antonio," she reminded him now, "but
I do know Johnny adored him."

"Is there an answer to my question there somewhere?" Jack asked impatiently.

She peered across the table at him with that funny
grin she used to give him in high school, more amused
by his impatience than annoyed. Then she extended her
hand, covered his and smiled reassuringly.

"There is, if you'll give me a chance to work up to it."

He frowned, feeling foolish, but equally entranced by
the sensation of her touch. She had beautiful hands, the
hands of an artist or a pianist. "Sorry. Go on."

"I told you Antonio essentially stole Johnny away
from Lillah. Besides getting him involved in the exclusive world of racing, he made himself a hero in the
boy's eyes by…telling him you'd abused his mother."

Jack muttered a curse. "Why the hell didn't Lillah set
him straight?"

Antonio's lies were understandable, if not forgivable,
but Jack was genuinely shocked that his ex-wife had
gone along. But then, she'd been unfaithful to him and
been willing to hurt him, though he didn't think she'd
ever done so intentionally. She was too self-absorbed to
think of other people, even her husband. He never

sensed she hated him or even had any particular animosity toward him. He just didn't satisfy her needs. Yet, as selfish as she was, it was one of the ironies of her personality that she didn't tell outright lies. When she had been confronted with her infidelity she didn't make any attempt to deny it. Lillah was willing to cheat, to take his son, even rob him of his pride, but she wouldn't lie to him.

"Because she didn't know until years after the damage was done. Antonio had made Johnny promise not to bring up the subject with his mother because it would upset her."

"The manipulative son of a bitch."

"She was incensed when she found out and tried to tell Johnny the truth, that she'd been the one who was unfaithful, but by then it was too late. Antonio convinced him she was making it all up because she didn't want to appear weak in his eyes, the helpless victim of domestic violence."

"And he bought that crap?" Jack muttered something unintelligible, picked up his wineglass and took a sip.

He wouldn't say it, but he was disappointed in his son. Surely at four he'd had enough of a memory of Jack to question Antonio's portrait of him—unless Lillah had already begun poisoning his mind before she took him away.

Raw anger surged through him. He set his wine back down on the table lest he crush the glass.

"She seems to have confided quite a lot to you," he said. "The Lillah I remember wasn't nearly as open about her feelings. Of course, that was a long time ago, and you're a woman."

"She was dying, Jack. That trumps self-delusion."

He shook his head sadly. "Maybe if she had—"

"Don't start the what-ifs. It's a game that inevitably leads to feeling sorry for yourself, and in the long run it accomplishes nothing."

He let out a small grunt. "Not just a woman. A philosopher. Don't worry about me, Megs. I won the poor-me contest a long time ago. Did my stint in the bottle, too."

She glanced at their half-full wineglasses and fingered the base of hers. "Should we be having this?"

Mirth warmed his chuckle this time. "I'm not an alcoholic. I was a drunk. They tell me there's a difference. Besides, my spate of inebriation lasted exactly one weekend. At the time, I couldn't afford the bar tab beyond that, plus the hangover cured any temptation to give my namesake Daniel's another shot at me."

She grinned. "You never could hold your liquor. Two beers was generally enough to have you curling up on the couch."

His eyes twinkled. "Still is. But I think we got off track. So Lillah told you about her abiding feelings for me."

HEARING THE SARCASM, Margaret looked at him carefully. After all these years Lillah's infidelity still hurt. Wounded male pride? He must have loved her once. Was his anger only because of losing his son or did he still feel something for the woman, as well? An unhappy thought came to mind. If Lillah's betrayal was so painful, what about Margaret's earlier rejection?

"She did better than tell me how she felt about you,

Jack. She gave me her diary, or rather diaries. There are three of them. The first is exclusively about your marriage and breakup. She comes across as pretty shallow and selfish and above all insensitive, something she later acknowledges. The second covers the middle years, her growing disillusionment with Antonio, her increasing awareness of her own culpability and sense of shame. The last volume can be best described as a memoir. Reminiscences. About life. About the mistakes she made. About you."

"Me?"

"After more than twenty years she'd come to realize how much she'd loved you—or could have if she'd given herself and you a chance. Having essentially lost her son, she finally understood the pain she'd inflicted on you. She had a lot of regrets."

Margaret studied the man sitting across from her, saw the confusion, the yearning to understand, the doubt. To finally learn the truth…

He'd said it would be small consolation, but that was before he really knew. She sensed relief rather than satisfaction, absolution rather than vindication.

"I brought them with me. They're in the car. I'll give them to you."

He stared blankly at her for a few seconds, as if the words had been spoken in a foreign language, then he slumped against the back of the booth. Another minute passed. He straightened.

"I don't want them."

"But—"

"She's dead, Megs. Let her rest."

Margaret studied him across the table, felt the ache she saw in his eyes, the pain he didn't want to acknowledge, the primal rage he was trying so hard to suppress.

"If you change your mind—"

"I won't."

"Jack, I'm sure she wanted you to read them. That's why she gave them to me, why she wanted to be brought back here to be buried. She wanted you and Johnny to finally be reunited. The diaries are her way of saying she's sorry."

"It's too late. The harm is done. You saw his reaction to me. He hates me. Nothing she says from the grave can make up for that."

The waiter brought their appetizers. Shrimp cocktail.

"Have you shown them to Johnny?"

She shook her head. "I felt you had a right to see them first."

"I don't want him to see them, either. Destroy them. Burn them."

"But why? He has a right to know you're not the—"

Jack shifted his jaw. "If Lillah had really wanted him to see them, she would have left them to him, not given them to you with some vague instruction to do with them what you thought was best."

He speared a shrimp. "I want them destroyed, Megs. If you won't do it, I will."

She frowned. "I'll take care of it. But I wish you'd tell me why you won't accept this peace offering, this gift, even belatedly."

He seemed frustrated by her plea, as if the explanation were patently obvious.

"From what you've told me, Johnny loved his mother, even if he didn't spend a lot of time with her."

"He loved her very much."

"Then leave it that way. He's lost the two people who meant anything to him. Leave him with his good memories."

"Even if they're lies…at your expense?"

He closed his eyes, opening them and took a sadness-filled breath. "Destroying their reputations won't make him love me. What's done is done and can't be unraveled. Let things be."

They ate, or rather nibbled at their appetizers in silence for several minutes.

"By the way," Margaret said after her second shrimp, "do you know how he died?"

Jack looked up. "Antonio? Heart attack is what I read."

"But not at home the way the media reported. He died in the bed of his mistress. When he collapsed, she called Lillah who arranged for the family's personal physician to go over to the woman's apartment. Antonio was already dead. The doctor had the body discreetly transported to the Rendisi villa so he could sign the death certificate there."

Jack stared at her. "Are you serious?"

"The doctor, the family chauffeur and a few house servants were well paid for their silence."

"Does Johnny know?"

"He helped the chauffeur bring the body back."

"My God."

The waiter poked his head around the corner. Jack skewered another shrimp to signal there was nothing wrong with the food. The waiter retreated.

"You said you were worried about Amber falling under Johnny's spell and being hurt the way Lillah was by Antonio," Jack reminded her. "Have you told her about the diaries?"

"It's been tempting, but I decided not to. For one thing, in her present frame of mind she probably wouldn't believe me, especially if Johnny denies it, and second, as much as I hate to admit it, I can't count on her discretion. The world doesn't need to know any more about the late Antonio Rendisi than it already does."

"I'm sorry—" the words were spoken softly "—you've been put in this difficult position."

"It's not your fault, Jack. None of it was ever your fault. I just wish you hadn't been the one who got hurt, first by me, then by Lillah."

"It was all a long time ago," he said.

But time didn't heal all wounds.

They finished the course in companionable silence, and the waiter brought their Caesar salads, which he topped with freshly grated pepper from an oversized mill.

"He was a good musician," Margaret said after her first bite of cold, crisp romaine lettuce, as if she had to justify herself. "Gary. He was better than most."

"And I had a tin ear." Jack laughed. "Still do, I guess. I know what I like when I hear it, but I can't tell you why, and if there's any pattern to my musical tastes, I don't have a clue what it is."

"Eclectic," she informed him, grinning. "Your tastes are eclectic."

He laughed again. "That sure sounds better than

common and unrefined. You used to play the piano. Do you still?"

She shook her head. "Haven't touched a keyboard in years. Gary pointed out that wanting to play wasn't enough, and even practice, when you don't have any talent, is a waste of time."

"Ouch."

She shrugged. "Unfortunately he was right. I'd talked my folks into piano lessons we couldn't afford because I loved watching Mrs. Whipplejohn play the ancient organ we had in our church with its tiered keyboards, all those mysterious stops and foot pedals. I wanted to be able to do that, too. It was fascinating to see both her hands and feet going at the same time and hear all that beautiful music come out." She laughed. "Trouble was I had absolutely no sense of rhythm and no talent. My teacher in kindergarten even took the triangle away from me because I couldn't keep time with the others."

"That's pretty bad," he agreed with a chuckle. "Still, you enjoyed playing. That should have been reason enough for you to keep at it, even if it was only for your own amusement."

"Too frustrating." She forked up a crouton. "I found more pleasure in appreciating other people's talents. Amber took up the violin for a while, was pretty good, too. But she lost interest after her father died."

Margaret sipped her wine, put the glass down.

"He could leach tears from a stone when he blew his horn," she went on, a little nostalgically. "In the best of times and in the worst I never got tired of hearing him play. He might have made a real name for himself, if he'd been willing to quit that loser combo he was in."

"Loyalty is a virtue," Jack reminded her.

"It can be," she acknowledged, "but not when it's blind or lazy. He was good at making the wrong decisions for what he always rationalized as the best reasons. He drank too much and got into drugs." Then she added, "And of course there were the women."

CHAPTER SEVEN

No "OF COURSE" ABOUT IT, Jack wanted to tell her, but she might misinterpret the remark as blaming her for not being able to satisfy her man. Hadn't he asked himself over and over if he had failed to excite Lillah enough? The fact was some people didn't appreciate a partner's love. For them there would always be another body to experience, another temptation to yield to. Antonio seemed to be such a man, and from all accounts, so was his son.

The waiter removed their salad plates and served the main course. Honey-glazed lamb chops for her. A thick tuna steak for him.

"How old was Amber when Gary died?"

"Sixteen."

"That's a difficult age to have to contend with the finality of death. Were she and Gary close?"

"She loved him, and in his own way he loved her. I often wished he'd spent more time with her, helped her develop her talent, for example, but violins don't have much of a role in jazz, except maybe in the blues, so he didn't pay as much attention to her musically as he would have if she'd chosen the clarinet or saxophone. Later I wondered what might have happened if he had.

Would he have been more stable or would she have become more unstable?"

"One of those unfathomable questions, Megs. Don't beat yourself up over it. I gather she took his death hard."

"Very. Then, shortly after he died, she started having problems. Initially our family doctor thought it was an emotional reaction to Gary's death. He prescribed antidepressants. She'd been a straight-A student until then, but the pills made it hard for her to concentrate. Her grades plummeted, and she didn't do at all well in her SATs. By then it was apparent the problem was physical."

Margaret paused. She'd already said more than she should have, more than she had intended. With anyone else she would have avoided this kind of candor, but with Jack it didn't seem necessary to hold back. It wasn't that she felt she owed him an explanation as much as confidence that she could be completely open with him. She'd been focusing on other people's needs for so long, it felt good to be able to express her own with him.

"Do you know what endometriosis is?" she asked.

"Some sort of female disorder," he said with a nervous shrug, avoiding eye contact, the way men often did at the mention of a woman's intimate anatomy.

Margaret almost smiled at his discomfort. "Close enough. It's quite painful and requires surgery. Amber was lucky. Her condition was relatively mild and uncomplicated, and her ability to have children hasn't been impaired, as far as we know. Nonetheless, follow-up treatment involves hormonal therapy."

Jack gazed at her questioningly.

"Birth control pills," she clarified.

This time he slowly nodded as the implication sank in. "All this happened before you received the invitation from Lillah?"

She nodded. "The timing seemed perfect. Amber had just gone through a miserable six months. The pain, the doctor's misdiagnosis, her doing so poorly in school at a critical time, the surgery and scare that she might never be able to have children. I figured getting away was what she needed, and to get to live in Italy! What could be better?"

Margaret cut into a lamb chop, dipped the piece in warm mint sauce.

"What you couldn't anticipate was her falling in love with Johnny."

"She doesn't have to worry about getting pregnant, and Johnny doesn't have to worry about her trapping him—"

"The way Lillah did me. Convenient for him."

A few minutes later the waiter came to clear their dishes away.

"Can I tempt you with some dessert?" He rattled off a list of items including bread pudding with Bourbon sauce.

"I've had it here before," Jack said. "It's fabulous." He quirked a brow playfully. "I'll split one with you."

Like old times when they'd shared food in restaurants. Back then, it had been because they couldn't afford to order two servings.

"I'm game," she said with a grin.

Jack put in the order "with two forks."

The waiter nodded and left.

"Johnny thinks he's going to whop my butt, doesn't he?" Jack asked, half in jest.

"That's his plan."

The return of the waiter was heralded by the tangy aroma of warm Bourbon. He put the bowl in the middle of the table between them. Presented each with forks, poured coffee and departed.

"Mmm." Margaret closed her eyes as she savored the first rich flavor of spices and raisins. "You were right. This is to die for."

Between them they demolished the dessert. Jack rested back against the booth seat and patted his flat belly. "That was good."

The waiter refilled their cups. After satisfied sips, Margaret asked, "Why didn't you ever go after him, Jack?"

"I did," he replied. "But think back, Megs. I was twenty-four years old and just starting out in the Busch Series. Yes, I was doing fairly well and was beginning to pick up some decent sponsors and win a few respectable purses, but I was hardly rich. I didn't have anything to speak of in savings, and Lillah had never been exactly frugal with our money."

He toyed with his spoon. "Still, I wasn't about to give up. Using money my folks really couldn't spare and what friends were able to lend me, I flew over to Italy a week after Lillah took off. I wasn't out for a big confrontation with her. By then I didn't care about her running out on me. I just wanted my son back."

He sipped his coffee. "It was a waste of time. The Rendisi family claimed they didn't know where Lillah was and refused to do anything to help me find her. They did tell me Antonio was in Melbourne, Australia, and from there was scheduled to continue on the Grand Prix circuit to Malaysia and Singapore."

He stared past her, feeling again the frustration of failure.

"There was no way I could afford to chase her around the world, so I was forced to come home. A few weeks later a letter arrived from an attorney in Switzerland notifying me she was filing for divorce. I can't tell you how much I wanted to fight for custody of Johnny, but I didn't have access to the kind of money I would have needed to challenge her in a European court. Lillah wasn't asking for alimony or child support. Be grateful for small favors, everybody said."

He took another sip of coffee, set the cup down. "When I got word that she'd married Rendisi, my first reaction was good riddance. I consoled myself with the satisfaction of knowing the bastard deserved what he was getting. Then came another notice, this one informing me Antonio Rendisi had petitioned an Italian court to formally adopt the boy and give him his name. Needless to say, I went ballistic."

Jack toyed with the handle of his cup and stared into the black brew, as if it had the secret answer to all his disappointments and failures.

Looking up, he said, "Again I wanted to fly over and contest it. My folks and friends were willing to help, but when I contacted a lawyer here I was hit with a tidal wave of cold water. I'd need an Italian attorney to plead my case in court over there, and I was told point-blank my chances of winning were tantamount to zero. Family and divorce courts in those days universally gave custody of children to their mothers, unless I could prove Lillah was a danger to the child, which I couldn't.

She was unfit as a wife, but despite all her complaining early on, I couldn't honestly say, much less prove, she wasn't a fit mother. That was the one thing I'd been hoping would save our marriage."

He stole another deep breath.

"I learned, too, that she and Rendisi had an ace up their sleeves. If they asserted in court that I'd been abusive or negligent, I would have to produce evidence and witnesses to counter their claims. Guilty until proven innocent. Where would I get the money to bring witnesses over to Italy or to pay Italian lawyers to file counterclaims and appeals that would probably drag on for years?"

Jack slumped against the booth's high back once again.

"My parents offered to sell their house to help cover expenses, but I couldn't let them do that. Pop had injured his back several years before, and while he was still able to work, he wasn't doing well. We weren't sure how much longer it would be before he was forced into retirement with not much more than Social Security disability to live on. Mom had a heart condition that required expensive medication. Besides, their house, which was where I was living again, wouldn't have brought enough for the bottomless pit of complicated legal battles I'd have to face. No way I could win.

"Ironically," he went on, "I also had to consider what would happen if I did win. I'd be totally broke, except now I'd have a young son to raise without a mother. My parents were more than willing to help, but poor health had made them older than their years and robbed them of the energy a growing young boy would have demanded. As it turned out, they were both dead within ten years."

Margaret reached across the table and touched his hand. "I'm sorry. I have fond memories of them."

"They always liked you." He savored the touch of her fingers on the back of his hand.

"What kind of life could I offer Johnny?" he asked. "We like to think love conquers all, but it doesn't pay bills, and I had to face the brutal fact that I'd be forever vulnerable. If Lillah and Rendisi really wanted to get my son away from me or just make my life miserable, he had the resources to pounce on the slightest perceived misstep on my part, and he could do it over and over again, ensuring I remained in constant debt, then using my poverty against me, to show I wasn't a good provider. Meanwhile Johnny would be the pawn, the tennis ball in our legal battles. I couldn't do that to my son."

Jack shook his head. "On the other hand, I had to consider the alternative. I've admitted Lillah was a decent mother. I paid for a detailed background investigation of Rendisi. I knew he was rich and from an old family. He had a reputation with women, but that was all before he met Lillah. There was nothing to indicate he'd played around since their marriage, absolutely nothing to suggest he was or would be anything other than a good father. He could certainly offer Johnny things I couldn't. Not then, at least. Not just wealth, but the opportunities old money can buy. A beautiful, ancestral home. A respected place in society. A good education."

Jack looked over at Margaret, his expression a plea for understanding. "The long and the short of it is I didn't give up on Johnny, at least not right away. Eventually I had to let him go for his own good. He'll never believe that, but it's the truth. If only Lillah had been willing to wait a little longer. A few years later I moved into the NASCAR NEXTEL Series and started making the kind of money Lillah wanted. I can't tell you how many times I reconsidered a fight, but each time I had to ask myself if it was the right thing to do for Johnny or if I was stroking my ego. I had to content myself with paying private investigative services to furnish me periodic reports about how he was doing."

"You kept track of him?"

"Of course I did. He's my son, Megs. I followed his progress in school, knew when he drove his first midget car, when he competed the first time—and lost. When he entered his first Formula 1 race. When he won the French Grand Prix. I caught a satellite interview he gave a couple of years ago in Paris and was blown away when I heard him speaking French like a native—" he grinned "—at least to my ear. My kid, speaking French and Italian. Amazing."

"German and Spanish, too," Margaret said. "But it must have been hard for you, watching him compete in auto racing and not being able to share it with him."

Jack paused for a second before answering. "Not a sharp pain anymore, as much as a chronic ache. I can still take pride in his achievements. I just have to do it privately—and from afar."

THE PARKING LOT was nearly empty, her car only a few spaces from his. Jack walked her to it, close enough for her to feel the energy emanating from him, close enough for his proximity to resonate in her. She was tempted to reach out and take his hand, but as much as they both might want it, neither of them was ready for that kind of contact yet, or the greater intimacy it promised. She leaned against the fender of her car and faced him.

"I'm sure you've gotten reports on him since he's been here," she said. "How's he doing?"

The hint of a smile crossed his lips. "Cal, my crew chief, has been keeping tabs on him for me through Mac Roberts, Steiner's crew chief. Apparently he's doing fairly well. Still having trouble adjusting to the tight groupings normal in NASCAR. They don't drive nearly as close together in open-wheel racing, but generally he seems to be doing all right." He chuckled. "Having a little trouble with the vocabulary, though. Keeps referring to refuelers instead of gas men, and he apparently blew everybody's mind the other day when he referred to the lollipop man."

"Lollipop man?" She laughed. "I can't imagine any self-respecting Southern boy wanting to be called a lollipop man."

Jack laughed with her. "He's the guy who stands directly in front of the car when it comes into the pit. He holds up—or I guess he holds down—a sign on a handle or stick, the lollipop, at the exact moment the driver is supposed to stop. When he's satisfied all the required actions have been completed, tire changes, refueling and so forth, he raises the lollipop as a signal to go. We don't have a similar position in NASCAR, but then Formula 1 has eleven people in their pit teams. We have only seven."

"I got to watch him race a couple of times with Lillah over in Europe. She pointed out some of the differences between NASCAR and Grand Prix, like jacking up the front and back of the car for tire changes instead of the sides the way we do."

"Did she still follow NASCAR?"

"Not closely, but she was aware of your record. She was proud of you, Jack."

He grunted. "Anyway, from all reports, Johnny's doing okay, been test-driving at a bunch of tracks across the country, trying to get a feel for banked ovals instead of the flat road courses he's used to. I think he's frustrated because things aren't going as smoothly or as quickly as he'd anticipated."

"You think he underestimated the challenge?"

"Probably. Playing paddleball and tennis look very similar, but I don't imagine being good at one necessarily means you'll be good at the other."

Odds were Johnny didn't want to admit what Jack did was as difficult or demanding as what he and his idol had done, either.

"He may or may not turn out to be a real competitor," Jack continued. "Steiner and his people apparently have mixed opinions about his potential."

"He won't give up easily," she declared.

"I'd be disappointed in him if he did."

A moment of silence followed. Rather than prolong their parting, Margaret said, "Thanks for a wonderful evening, Jack. The food was fabulous, but the company was better."

"We've talked so much about me, I haven't asked

about you. Are you going back to nursing again, now that you're home?"

"Lillah left me a very generous bequest, far more than I deserve or ever anticipated. I don't have to work now. But I enjoy nursing, so I'll probably return to it. For now, though, I think it's important for me to be available for Amber."

He shifted his weight. "Look, over the next couple of months I'll be spending a lot of time out of town," he said. "But not all of it. When I'm here…if you can stand my company, I'd like to call you, see if we might be able to get together…for dinner."

She raised her hand to his cheek. "I'd like that."

CHAPTER EIGHT

OVER THE THREE-MONTH hiatus between the mid-November end of one NASCAR racing season and the mid-February beginning of the next, Jack was kept busy making personal appearances, promoting products, negotiating contracts with agents and sponsors, as well as planning strategies and tactics with Cal and the rest of his team. But whenever he was back in Greensboro, he called Margaret and took her out to dinner. He was already booked as a featured guest on a Caribbean cruise over Christmas, an annual tradition for him. He invited her to come along, but she declined. She'd never been on a cruise and would like to take one some day, but not at Christmas. For her the holiday was about home, the smell of cooking and the closeness of family, not a crowd of strangers on the warm Caribbean Sea. Besides, she didn't want to leave Amber and didn't think the occasion would be very merry if she came along.

Johnny flew back to Italy several times to attend to business and estate matters there. Amber was disappointed when he didn't invite her to go with him, especially over the Christmas holidays, but she was smart enough not to harp on it or pout in his presence. In the

States he spent most of his time with Vaughn Steiner's team members and traveled across the country to study NASCAR tracks. Amber went with him sometimes, but not nearly as often as she would have liked.

Margaret used the same time to get her own affairs in order. When she'd gone to Europe with Amber she'd arranged through a real estate agent to lease out her house. The place was again vacant when they returned and they moved back in, but Margaret found it far shabbier looking than she remembered and set about getting it repaired and renovated.

"Why not sell the place as is, Mom?" Amber asked. This was one of her crabbier days, when she couldn't seem to sit still, complained about everything and generally made a disagreeable nuisance of herself. "With the bequest you got from Lillah we can afford much bigger and better."

That was certainly true, but it irritated Margaret that her daughter seemed so willing to abandon the house she'd grown up in without a backward glance.

"I mean, it's not like this is some ancestral palace." *Ah, like the Rendisi villa outside Florence.* "It's a dinky little dump in a lousy neighborhood."

Margaret couldn't deny the area wasn't as nice as it had once been, but she was offended that her daughter felt no emotional attachment for what Margaret had worked so hard to make an attractive and comfortable home.

"Because it's my money, Amber, and I'll do with it what I want."

Amber shrugged, unconvinced.

Margaret had the necessary repairs done, as well as a few of the obvious renovations that would make the place more saleable while she started house hunting. Her evenings were spent hitting the books in preparation for her nursing recertification.

"Why do you even bother, Mom?" Amber asked again. "You don't have to work anymore."

"I can't sit around doing nothing, honey. Besides, I enjoy nursing. I like helping people."

Amber turned up her nose. "Whatever."

Margaret was infuriated and puzzled by her daughter's cavalier attitude. The mood swings were beginning to worry her. For days she'd be sweet and helpful, talk about going to college or putting in more hours at her part-time job as a waitress so she could save money and be independent—then overnight she'd dismiss it all as a waste of time and energy. Margaret had been searching for a pattern in her daughter's behavior, but she hadn't been able to find any.

"There was a time when you liked helping people, too," she said. "What's happened, honey? All you seem to care about anymore is yourself."

And Johnny.

"Why don't you go back to school, Amb? You'll appreciate it a lot more after spending a year in Europe."

Amber lethargically paged through a fashion magazine. "I don't know what I want to study," she said without looking up.

"Sign up for some classes and find out," Margaret nearly shouted. She calmed herself. "You don't have to major in anything right away. Freshman year is to find out what's available, what subjects you're interested in." She let out a huff of frustration. "If you don't want to go to college, get a full-time job, so you can start earning decent money."

"Why?" Amber challenged. "Lillah left us plenty."

"Left *me*, Amber. It's *my* money to do with as *I* please. It's not yours. You need to get off your duff and earn your own way, do something useful instead of lazing around here from morning to night."

Unfazed by the outburst, Amber replied, "When the racing season starts I won't have time to work. I'll be traveling around with Johnny."

"If he lets you."

"Don't be silly. Of course he will, Mom."

Margaret fumed. There was an alternative to letting her daughter leech off her, but it hardly seemed better. If only she could figure out what was making her little girl so irresponsible.

The next time Jack called to invite her out to eat, she suggested he come to her house for a home-cooked meal. Dining out was lovely. The food was inevitably good and it was nice being waited on, but home was where one relaxed.

Amber knew only Johnny's side of the story about Jack and in total loyalty to him refused to consider he might be wrong. But Amber would be out that evening—with Johnny. Jack would be long gone by the time Johnny brought her home.

"How's the house hunting going?" Jack asked as he pulled the cork on the bottle of white wine Margaret had removed from the refrigerator. She'd chosen a semidry white to go with the honey-and-rosemary glazed chicken roasting in the oven.

She told him about the various places she'd seen, the apartments, the condos, the houses, what she liked about each and what she didn't.

"I need a place big enough so Amber will feel comfortable living there, but that isn't so big I'll rattle around in it when she finally moves out."

"Buy big now and downsize later," Jack suggested.

"That makes sense, I suppose. It's just that I've moved so rarely that relocating is a big deal for me, and I don't relish the prospect of going through it repeatedly."

Jack laughed. "With me it's the opposite. I've moved around so much the idea of staying in one place for very long gives me claustrophobia." He poured their wine and brought her a glass. Handing it over, he said, "But moving isn't the real problem. Tell me what is."

Was it right to unload on him? After holding so much back for so long, it would feel incredibly good to share it with someone. Not someone. With Jack. Their time together was becoming very precious to her. More than a pleasant evening with an old friend should.

She turned down the oven temperature to warm. The food would be ready to serve whenever they wanted it. A little extra time wouldn't harm anything. Margaret waved Jack to the sitting area. He took the couch. She chose the love seat. They turned to face each other.

After a sip of wine she told him about her problems with Amber, about her daughter's apathetic attitude, her lack of ambition. He listened patiently and waited a minute before responding.

"Maybe it's time for tough love, Megs. Playing nice doesn't seem to work anymore. Give her a deadline when she has to leave, then follow through on it."

She closed her eyes for a couple of seconds and nodded. "In principle I agree with you, but here's my dilemma. She has a high school education, but no college credits, no job skills to speak of. She can get minimum-wage jobs, but not much more, not with her attitude. Where is she going to live? Under what conditions? She's prime victim material, Jack. I could never live with myself if—"

"What about Johnny?"

"Oh, I have no doubt she'd go crying to him, and knowing him he'll take her in, but what will that accomplish? Yes, it'll keep her off the streets, but will it make her a better person?"

"Only she can do that. You can give her the tools and the opportunities, but she has to decide to use them."

"I'm sure you're right, but..." She bit her lips.

He got up and walked around the coffee table. Sitting beside her he wrapped her in his arms. She stiffened at first, then, as if by instinct, as if she had been waiting for him forever, she curled into his embrace. A moment later the tears started. She struggled to hold them back.

"It's all right, Megs," Jack said softly in her ear. "Let it out. I'm here. I'm not going away." He stroked her back, soothed her with gentle hands that felt strong and tender, the hands of someone who cared about her.

It had been so long since anyone had held her. She pressed herself against him, fearful that if she didn't he would vanish.

She raised her head and before she knew it his lips were on hers. Tentative at first, then in a flash they both deepened the kiss. Her blood raced. Her fingers dug into his back. He pulled her tighter against his chest. She could feel his heart pounding.

She knew what the next step was, and she wanted to go there. Longed to. Ached to. Her entire body was crying out. The bedroom was but a few steps away.

But sensible Margaret pulled back.

Sensible Margaret considered the consequences. Her daughter wasn't there but she could come flying through the door at any time. Suppose… What if…

She rested her head against Jack's chest. Yes, she could hear his heartbeat. She could feel the tension in his posture, the heat of his body.

She gazed up into his eyes, saw his need, his desire. "Thank you for being here," she said lamely.

His smile was strained. "My pleasure."

Reluctantly, shakily, she removed herself from his embrace and all but staggered back to the kitchen area. As if moving in slow motion, she opened the oven to check its contents and had to stop and concentrate on what she was doing.

"Everything's ready," she said too brightly a moment later.

"Let me help."

Neither said anything as together they placed bowls and dishes on the already set table. She arranged the chicken pieces on a platter while Jack lit the two candles in their crystal holders.

He complimented her on the food. Toasted the chef with his wine. For the first time in years, she blushed.

"Still planning to go back to nursing?" he asked sometime later.

"I don't think I was made for a life of leisure."

"We agree on that," he commented. "How many times can you read fashion magazines?"

She laughed. Many times, if Amber was any indication. "I think I'm going to specialize in care for the terminally ill."

"Like hospice?" he asked. "It's a wonderful calling, but it's got to be awfully draining emotionally."

She'd thought a lot about this. "Over the years I've seen my share of patients die, and like all medical people I regarded their deaths as defeat. But being with Lillah in those last weeks and days taught me death is not failure. It's the natural end of life, and being there for those final moments… This probably doesn't make much sense, but being present for those last moments took the sting out of death. It's not so scary anymore."

She paused, certain he didn't understand. "I've talked to half a dozen end-of-life caregivers, and they all say the same thing, that the rewards outweigh the sadness."

He reached across the table and took her hand. "Then do it."

Were the table not between them she was sure he would have kissed her then. As it was she had to be content with the warmth of his hand and the gentle caress she found in his eyes.

"Lillah, it seems, has inspired you," he observed. "I doubt it's the kind of influence she ever expected to have, but I'm glad she has. It makes up for some of the other things."

Margaret served dessert—homemade tapioca pudding. He smiled when she presented it. "This is still my favorite, but I haven't had it in years." She smiled as she poured coffee and they moved to the couch.

The conversation turned to Johnny, as Margaret knew it inevitably would. Jack wanted every detail she could furnish about him. She recounted some of her past conversations with him, his remarks, attitudes, how he'd asked about his mother's parents when they were going to the cemetery.

"But not about me or my folks?"

She shook her head. "It's like he's made a conscious decision not to."

Maybe, Margaret mused, she shouldn't have made the last comment, but what would be the point of holding back? If Jack was ever going to be reunited with his son, he had to know all the facts.

"Let me talk to him, Jack. Let me give him the diaries."

He shook his head emphatically from side to side. "You said you'd destroy them."

She put down her cup. "I will, if that's what you really want, but—"

"I told you why I don't want him to see them."

"It's wrong for you to take all the blame. He has a right to know—"

"Why can't you understand? Ruining his memories of her isn't going to make him like me. If my kid is as smart as you say he is, he's already aware—whether he's willing to admit it or not—that Antonio was a lying, cheating, manipulative bastard. But he'll resent me all the more if I take away his mother, as well."

"I think you're underestimating him, Jack."

"Destroy the damn things, Megs. Please. You mentioned his grandmother's quilting. I think I may have a better way to wake him up, to stir memories."

They heard a key in the front door. He and Margaret both climbed to their feet.

"I didn't expect them home for another couple of hours," she muttered.

Jack winked at her. "At least they've caught us with our clothes on."

Margaret giggled and still had a guilty smile on her face when they turned and stood side by side, facing the two people who walked in and stopped dead in their tracks.

"What's he doing here?" Amber asked.

"I beg your pardon?" Margaret shot back. "This happens to be my house."

The two younger people continued to stare at them.

"I understand you're planning to compete in the NASCAR NEXTEL Series," Jack said to his son.

"What I do is none of your business," Johnny replied sharply.

"My, my. What ever happened to the smooth European sophistication I've heard so much about?" Margaret asked. "There must be something in the water over here. It brings out the crass incivility in even the most well-mannered foreigners."

"I'll be going," Jack said graciously.

"I don't blame you," Margaret said in an apologetic tone.

"Dinner was delicious. Thank you." He leaned over and gave her a chaste peck on the cheek. "Good night."

As he passed his son, he said, "See you in Daytona."

MEETING JACK'S CREW at Daytona was for Margaret like going back in time. Not the sights so much. NASCAR's clean, shiny, gaudily decaled cars were pristine and far more glamorous than the ones Jack and his friends had played with when they were in high school. The surroundings were much different, too. No lumpy-bumpy dirt tracks that turned into muddy quagmires in the rain. No improvised shade-tree mechanics shops or dented, battered chaotic tool chests, either. Here everything was as neat and precise as a surgical suite.

It was the sounds that initially took her back to her teenage years. Loud, grumbling, harsh and nerve-shattering. The reverberations were deeper now and somehow more confident, but essentially the same. Brute energy. Explosive power.

What hadn't changed at all were the smells. Raw fuel, oil, lubricants, hot asphalt and burned rubber.

If she closed her eyes she was a teenager again, her whole body resonating to the guttural timbre of throbbing engines. In her mind's eye she saw Jack in permanently stained, knee-worn, shredded jeans, his callused hands black with grease. A faded, threadbare T-shirt stretched across his thick-muscled chest, banding his bulging biceps. Dark hair winged down over his forehead, giving only momentary glimpses of his vibrantly clear blue eyes.

Most of all she could picture the pensive, serene smile on his lips as he contemplated the latest problem, the latest technical crisis to be resolved.

The world of internal combustion engines, gears and speed had been his life then. It still was.

His fingernails were clean now. No more grease or carbon smudges on his cheeks. Yet the gleam in his eye was no less bright with the pure, rapturous joy of being with these big machines.

"I'm pleased to finally meet you," Caleb Farnsworth said, when Jack introduced them in the garage bay at the Daytona track.

She took his extended hand and felt her own swallowed up in it. "I've heard a lot about you." Jack had called him his best friend and said that he'd told him about Lillah, about Johnny. She hadn't gotten a chance to find out how much more he knew.

"Some of it good, I hope."

"Mostly that you're old," she said deadpan.

He gaped at her, dumbstruck for a second, glanced at the smug grin on Jack's face, then broke into a guffaw. "Old, huh?"

"Oh, and wise," she added with a coy smile.

He continued to chuckle with amusement. "I can't imagine Jack ever calling me wise, but I like the little white lies you tell, lady."

"I think the term I used was wiseass," Jack contributed.

"Come on, fibber—" Cal patted Margaret's hand as he tucked it in the crook of his arm "—let me show you around." He turned to Jack. "You can go now, sonny."

Jack's eyes twinkled. "I have a meeting with Habersham. Not sure how long I'll be, but I'll find you when it's over," he told Margaret. "If you're real good, old-timer," he said to his friend, "I'll let you join us for lunch."

He strolled off, and Cal proceeded to show Margaret around and introduce her to members of the team.

"I'm glad you've come back into his life," Cal said some minutes later, as they stood outside the entrance to the bay, watching stock cars rumble by. "He needs someone right now who understands what he's been through, what he's still going through with that boy of his. This isn't exactly the homecoming he'd envisioned."

"There's a lot Johnny doesn't understand."

"And Jack won't force the truth on him."

She looked over at him, unsure exactly what the crew chief meant.

"He told me about the diaries," he explained.

"Then maybe you can convince him Johnny needs to see them."

"So you haven't destroyed them yet?"

Caught. She'd told Jack she would, twice, but they were too valuable. They held the truth, or at least a different version of the truth than the one Johnny believed.

She shook her head.

They saw Jack striding toward them down the alley between the long row of garages.

"Don't give up on him," Cal said. "He'll come around. Reluctantly, maybe kicking and screaming, but he wants his son back even more than he wants to save his pride."

FRIDAY WAS CHAOS. The opening race of the season had everyone on edge. As hyped as he was himself, Jack couldn't help smiling at Cal running around in a frenzy. Daytona, the gauntlet of the nine-month season was the only time his crew chief got strung out. No second chance to make a good first impression, he would tell his team. No doubt about it, but Jack had learned a long time ago that in the final analysis it was immaterial.

True, everybody looked to the opening competition to get a feel for what the rest of the season might hold. Daytona was prestigious. Winning was a good omen for people who were superstitious, who believed in signs and premonitions. The fact remained, however, that Daytona was just one of more than three dozen races that would be run on nearly two dozen different tracks over the course of the next nine months. Points earned at this track weren't any more valuable than points earned anywhere else, and in the end it all came down to who earned the most points.

Still, there was a lot to be said for first impressions.

Not too far down the wide concrete lane separating the long rows of garages, Jack caught occasional glimpses of Johnny's team and his black-and-silver Ford with the number 581 on its side. Midbar Resorts, his main sponsor, was emblazoned across the hood.

Oh, to be a fly on the wall, Jack thought.

Johnny hadn't run his qualifying lap yet, but Cal's informants were reporting he hadn't done well in his trials. No one seemed to know why. Formula 1 courses were far more complex and theoretically, at least, more challenging than stock car oval tracks. They had more twists and all the turns weren't left, nor were they always as banked as NASCAR tracks were. This oval should be a piece of cake for an experienced Formula 1 driver.

Was Johnny spooked by the unfamiliarity of the setting? Not likely. Jack knew he'd been practicing on other tracks for months. It didn't seem plausible that he'd be intimidated by this one or by the competitors he was up against.

It had to be the car. So what was wrong with it? Steiner Racing was as good as any outfit in the NASCAR NEXTEL Cup Series. They knew how to build engines, assemble chassis, and their pit crews were among the fastest and most dependable in the business.

Bad karma?

Or maybe just an inexperienced team that hadn't yet gotten its act together.

"You're on deck." Cal's voice came through in the headset of Jack's helmet.

He went through his mental checklist. After all these years he'd learned never to take anything for granted. Racing might appear easy to the uninformed observer, but as in so many sports, appearances could be deceiving. Part of a professional's expertise was making the difficult look easy.

The needles of the gauges on his dashboard all quivered precisely where they should.

He gunned the engine. The ear protection furnished by the tight-fitting helmet muffled most of the sound, but he didn't have to hear the totality of its full-volume roar to know the engine was in perfect tune. He could feel it. Racing employed all the senses: sight, sound, smell, touch, sometimes even taste. Maybe that was one of the reasons it was so all-consuming and produced an adrenaline rush that lasted for hours over hundreds of miles, a rush that never lost its appeal.

"Next up."

Another scan of the dashboard. Nothing had changed, though his sense of urgency had climbed to fever pitch.

"Go, go, go, go, go!"

The rear end swerved. Smoke billowed from spinning tires, the acrid stench of burning rubber assailed his nostrils. Most of all he felt that tingling in his body as he pulled g's on his way down the straightaway.

At two and a half miles, the Daytona track was one of the longest on the circuit. Only Talladega was longer. Their high-banked turns also made them the fastest, allowing speeds in excess of 200 miles per hour.

For that reason engines were hobbled with restrictor plates, which limited the volume of air and fuel that flowed into the carburetor, thereby reducing speed and power. Instead of decreasing excitement of the races, however, restrictor plates heightened it, as drivers fought all the harder for position.

It was another four hours before the results were officially known, but when they were, even Cal couldn't hide a wide grin of satisfaction.

Jack had won the pole, the first position on the inside of the double line of cars. Definitely a good start.

He reviewed the list of the fifty-seven cars that had competed for qualification. Only forty-three could make the cut. The Number 581 car, Johnny's, was in twenty-ninth position. Not bad for a rookie, though he suspected his boy was far from pleased with it. Grand Prix drivers justifiably placed a good deal of emphasis on their starting positions. Getting the pole often equated to winning the race, since passing was infrequent and dangerously difficult in open-wheel racing. The important thing, however, was that Johnny had made the cut. He was in the race.

Jack was walking through the garage area on his way to his motor home when he passed Steiner's bay. He and Vaughn went back more than a dozen years together, and Jack had to admit he was disappointed his old rival was no longer racing. The shoulder injury that had kept him out of competition for two years had reportedly been repaired in surgery following another accident, neither of which had been track related, but word was that his therapist had recommended he sit out one more season. For the two-time NASCAR NEXTEL Cup winner being a mere observer on the sidelines must be pure torture.

Johnny sauntered out of the bay, apparently unaware Jack was passing by. The two men nearly collided. For a moment they stared at each other, both with their shoulders defensively high.

Jack was first to lower his. "Congratulations on qualifying today."

Johnny said nothing.

Jack offered a thin smile, stepped around his son and continued on his way. He imagined someone would explain to the new kid on the block that good sportsmanship dictated the courtesy of a polite reply.

Sam Collins, the engine specialist for the team next

to Steiner's, called out, "Nice going, Jack. Congratulations on taking the pole."

Jack raised his right hand. "Thanks," he said and moved on.

CHAPTER NINE

"NILS BOOKER JUST BOUNCED off the wall on Turn Two," Cal reported in Jack's ear. "Open on the inside."

Two seconds later Jack was there, Jem Nordstrom close behind, squeezing through the bottleneck.

"Yellow flag," Cal said. The field was now frozen in place as the mess Booker had created was being hurriedly cleaned up.

Jack did some quick calculations. He was in the lead with seven laps to go. He'd had a pit stop twenty-two laps back and could definitely use a gas-and-go now to be on the safe side, but then he'd have to yield his position, and it was too late in the game for that. Several of the guys who were at the back of the pack had pulled off onto pit road for a quick refill, but Jack's main challengers in the front had not. Did he have enough fuel to finish the race?

The caution flag, often a savior when fuel was low, now complicated things. He was burning precious gas and getting nowhere. On the other hand, low fuel also meant lighter weight. He discussed the situation with Cal.

"Your call," his crew chief finally said. Great help!

"I'm going for it," Jack replied.

His logic was simple. Pull in and he would lose first place for sure. Stay out on the track and he could run his tank dry…or he just might win. A chance was better than a certainty in this case. There were no guarantees. Not in this sport.

They circled the field three more times before the yellow flag was dropped. All clear. Four laps to go.

Jack jammed his right foot to the fire wall and shot forward. Jem Nordstrom was on his bumper all the way. That was to both their advantages. The draft, the long slip-stream the two of them formed, gave them greater speed together than they would have gotten separately and provided greater distance from the pack behind them. In this case, though, it also worked to Jack's disadvantage, because the continuous flow of air above the two combined vehicles took the downward pressure off the spoiler on his trunk lid, making his tail loose and less con-trollable. A small tap on his rear bumper would be enough to destabilize him, send him whirling to the right, as cen-trifugal force pulled him to the outside of the track. This afforded the guy behind him the crucial seconds he needed to slingshot around him on the inside and take the lead.

It was called a bump-draft, and it was very effective— if used by an experienced driver. It had its dangers, though. A slam rather than a tap could send the lead car careening sideways down the middle of the track or flying up against the outside wall, resulting in a crash, a rebound and maybe a pileup of the cars behind him. Jack had the consolation of knowing Jem Nordstrom had been racing a long time and was an ace at handling contingencies.

Three laps to go. The draft had put the two of them

at least six car lengths ahead of the pack and four ahead of their nearest competitor.

Two laps to go. Now was when Nordstrom would make his move.

Jack shimmied to the right. Not far. Only enough to break the draft without giving Nordstrom adequate space to slide up on the inside. Spectators wouldn't notice it, but Jack instantly felt his speed decrease by several miles per hour.

Turn One coming up.

Jack hugged the inside, then ratcheted to the right sufficiently to foil an outside shot. Jem, thinking or at least hoping, Jack would move farther out, stayed as close to the inside line as he could, but there wasn't enough room to pass and time was running out.

On Turn Two Jack drifted back in, then out again, frustrating Jem. No draft, and a bump at these speeds could destroy them both.

Straightaway. Cat and mouse. Jack didn't need a draft now. He and Jem were well ahead of the pack.

But would his fuel hold out?

Jack continued to wiggle back and forth, never giving Jem the inside lane, denying him the bump that would propel Jack up against the outside wall.

Turn Three.

Turn Four.

Straightaway.

The checkered flag. The crowd waved and roared.

Jack had taken Daytona.

If he believed in omens, this would be a very good season indeed. First the pole position. Then Victory Lane.

Sweet.

He ran out of gas on his victory lap. Nothing else to do but sit there and grin as his car coasted powerless to a dead stop. What could be more perfect?

He waved to the crowd in the stands, gave them a cheerful thumbs-up as he was getting an emergency shot of fuel. He had a question he wanted to ask Cal, but there were too many people monitoring the radio. It would have to wait.

Over the next two hours he was absorbed by the all-consuming energy and pageantry of victory. Climbing out of the stifling vehicle, spraying everyone with champagne, the endless interviews with the media, the presentation of awards and expressions of gratitude to all the people who made it possible. More media attention. It was heady stuff.

Some would say it was the reason drivers raced, but Jack knew the explanation was only partially true. The real reason race car drivers raced was for the pure thrill of speed and daring, for the adrenaline rush of hitting 180 miles per hour plus, of constantly skirting danger and prevailing against it. Whether there was a Victory Lane or not, men—and women—would still race. Call it a metaphor for life. Call it the ultimate reality show, but be it climbing Everest or running a marathon, people would embrace a challenge. The champions weren't necessarily the winners; the real champs were the ones who could later say "I did it," the individuals who loved what they did when they were doing it. Nobody could ever take that joy away.

The pageantry over, the adrenaline high subsiding, soon to be replaced by total exhaustion, Jack was finally let loose long enough to go back to his motor home, peel himself out of his sweat-soaked uniform and take a long cool shower. First, though, he asked Cal, "How did Johnny do?"

"Came in twenty-ninth. Right where he started."

Jack offered a thin smile. "He's probably not very happy with that."

Cal snorted. "First race? Hell, I'm impressed he even finished."

So am I, Jack thought, but he said nothing as he made his way to that refreshing shower.

RENDISI WAS IN A MOOD. Steiner understood why. He'd entered the race to win, not to stand still, which is essentially what he'd done by finishing in the same position he'd started. Especially disappointing when that place was toward the back of the pack. From Steiner's perspective Rendisi hadn't done badly. At least he hadn't lost ground, but that wasn't good enough for a guy who saw himself as *The Champ*. Which, in Vaughn's estimation, was part of the problem.

NASCAR and Formula 1 were about as similar as bagels and doughnuts. What didn't help was that Rendisi had a tendency to look down on NASCAR as a sort of poor man's Grand Prix, which it definitely was not. As a result he'd gone into his qualification round feeling cocky, convinced he, international racing star, had the world by the tailpipe.

That was his first mistake. His second was letting himself be distracted by the poor showing. His third? Well, the kid had a lot to learn about close-quarter racing.

"You held your ground," Steiner said, as they watched his car, not a scratch on it, being loaded into the overhead compartment of the hauler. "That's not a bad beginning."

Johnny only grunted.

Funny, the guy could be the epitome of charm when things were going his way. The press certainly doted on him, as did his new fans, especially the women. But he could also be moody as hell. Steiner had recently gone through a rough spot in his own life and hadn't been ideal company, so he understood the seduction of self-pity, but he'd also learned that a positive attitude was infectious and self-fulfilling.

"Relax tonight," Steiner consoled, "then tomorrow sit down and watch the race on TiVO. Pay particular attention to Jack Dolman. His winning today wasn't dumb luck. Study his technique. Check out what he does and when he does it. Some of his moves are blatant, the kind anyone in his position would make, but he can also be subtle as hell. The guy's got a sixth sense for the world around him, seems to be able to get into the heads of the other drivers and anticipate their moves. He's one of the best drivers I know for playing the outside, staying detached, biding his time. Then all of a sudden he moves in and before anyone realizes what's happening, he's in front. He drove a near perfect race today. You can learn a lot from him."

Studying the winner was common sense, but instead of embracing the advice, Johnny's frown only deepened.

"He started off in the pole position," he pointed out.

"It certainly helped," Steiner acknowledged, "and I

realize in Grand Prix racing you put a lot of weight on opening positions, but this is NASCAR, not Grand Prix, Johnny. Starting position is important, but it's not crucial."

In Formula 1 drivers ran two qualifying rounds on two consecutive days, the combined speeds of the two determining the lineup order. The first round was for raw speed with minimum fuel. The second was more calculated, because immediately afterward the car was locked up for the night in a guarded cantonment area and not allowed to refuel until the first pit stop of the race the following day.

"We do a lot more passing at much closer tolerances in NASCAR than you do in open-wheel racing," Steiner reminded him, then, to lighten the moment, he threw up his hands and laughed. "Hell, you know all that. Look, despite what you may think right now, you did well today. I've had a lot more experience in this than you have, so trust me on this. You did fine." He rested his right hand on his newest driver's shoulder. "Study the Number 424 car. Dolman's the driver you want to model yourself on."

Johnny nodded and started to move away.

"See you in California on Thursday," Steiner called out.

"Yeah," Johnny muttered and kept moving. "See you in California."

Steiner stood there a minute and watched the rookie trudge toward his million-dollar motor home. There was something about the guy that didn't sit right, but Steiner couldn't figure out what it was. Arrogance, definitely. But arrogance and overconfidence went hand in glove with many high achievers and certainly weren't unusual with successful sportsmen and athletes. It was a corollary of confidence, or some would say the flip side of insecurity. Bagels and doughnuts again. No matter how many Grand Prix trophies Rendisi had won, he was still a rookie in NASCAR.

And why did he almost flinch at the mention of Dolman's name?

CHAPTER TEN

JOHNNY MADE HIS WAY BACK to his motor home. Steiner undoubtedly had good intentions in recommending he watch Jack Dolman's tactics in winning the race. He had no idea he was rubbing salt into a wound. But it was advice Johnny would have to take if he was going to beat the man. More than anything, Johnny wanted to defeat—humiliate—the man who had abused his mother and abandoned him.

Amber was waiting for him inside. She'd changed from the modest attire Steiner's people had insisted she wear around the infield and garage area for something more provocative. A clinging top with a low neckline that revealed a tantalizing glimpse of cleavage. A bare midriff that exhibited the new gold ring in her navel. Snug shorts that exposed long, perfectly toned legs.

The woman was stacked, no question about it. Johnny just couldn't figure out why lately she seemed to feel this compulsion to put herself on display. What she didn't seem to comprehend was that she had natural elegance when she was simply being herself. She certainly didn't have to tart herself up to get men to notice her.

Johnny had never met a woman like Amber. She had

a sweet and gentle side that brought out a part of him even he hadn't been aware of. His better nature? His own vulnerability? All he knew was that with Amber there was a push-pull between them he didn't fully understand, a dichotomy that tantalized him and frightened him at the same time.

She came up to him now, entwined her fingers behind his neck, pressed herself against him and kissed him on the lips. The warmth of her curves produced an automatic response. Without thinking he coiled his arms around her waist and deepened the kiss. Aggressively she ratcheted it up yet another notch.

He broke off, almost forcefully, and removed her hands from his neck. "Amber, are you high on something?"

The thought had entered his mind before, but other than her crazy moods, he'd never found any evidence she was using drugs, and she always vehemently denied it.

She screwed up her face with annoyance. "Of course not."

"You better not be." He didn't detect any liquor on her breath. "I've warned you before, and I'm warning you now. No drugs. You trip out and get caught, you're on your own. I can't afford to be associated with a junkie."

"Why are you always picking on me?" She stomped her foot and turned away. "I told you I don't do drugs. You think I'm stupid?"

"No," he replied, "I don't think you're stupid, and I'm not picking on you, honey. I'm just telling you—"

"Yeah, yeah. I know what you're telling me. You don't give a hoot about me. It's always all about you and your precious career."

"That's not true, *cara*. I don't want you to get hurt. I care too much about you, *bellissima*."

That did it, as he knew it would. She let out a sigh of frustration, then instantly transformed herself into the bright, chipper flirt she'd been a minute before, again making him wonder if she was on something.

"I watched the whole race," she said. "You really scared me when you kept getting boxed in, but you didn't let them touch you. Awesome."

He stepped to the refrigerator and opened it.

"Hardly," he muttered over his shoulder. He removed a sports drink from the inside of the door, twisted off the orange cap and took a long draw.

"Disappointed?" Margaret asked as she moved up to the marble counter from the living area.

Johnny jumped, almost spilling the drink. He hadn't realized she was there, which meant she'd seen her daughter practically maul him, overheard their exchange. Talk about embarrassing.

"Of course he is, Mom," Amber replied irritably for him. "He didn't win."

"Thanks for rubbing it in."

Margaret addressed him directly. "Actually, I think you did pretty darn well out there today."

He snorted. "Uh-huh. How do you figure that?" He tipped the bottle back and took another gulp.

"You qualified."

"Nowhere near the pole."

"You finished."

"Where I started."

"And you didn't lose any ground."

He peered over at her, trying to decide if she was praising him or mocking him.

He liked Margaret, and he certainly appreciated what she'd done for his mother. The two women were so different it was hard to imagine them coming from the same background. Margaret didn't have the social sophistication and grace that his mother had, but she made up for it with an artless sincerity that garnered respect. He'd watched her take her cue from other people at the dinner table before selecting the appropriate fork, wait for other guests to choose their aperitifs before requesting hers, but only the first time. She had enough self-confidence to carry on from there.

"Of the forty-three cars that started today," Margaret elaborated, "six wiped out and didn't finish and seventeen finished farther back in the pack from where they started. So I'd say all things considered you had a darn good day for your first-ever NASCAR race."

"Where did you hear all that, Mom?"

"I didn't hear it anywhere, Amber. I watched the race."

"And you kept track of that stuff in your head?"

Margaret crooked an eyebrow at Johnny and curled her lips in amusement, then spoke to her daughter. "What, you don't think your old lady is smart enough to figure out what's going on?"

Johnny snickered, uncomfortably aware of the double entendre in her words. Amber retreated into silence.

He doubted she'd made much of an attempt today to follow what was happening on the track beyond finding his car in the pack. Margaret's perceptiveness, on the other hand, impressed him. She obviously knew something about NASCAR, but then, by her own admission, she'd been Jack Dolman's girlfriend before he took up with his mother. Margaret claimed she'd dumped him, but Johnny wondered if she wasn't trying to save face, just as his mother had in denying Jack's abuses, rather than admit that she, too, had been victimized. Like Lillah.

Maybe not. He remembered her running to catch up with Jack at the cemetery, their talking briefly before she returned to the group and Jack drove off. He'd heard rumors of them meeting in restaurants after that, and there had been the evening he'd brought Amber home early because she was complaining of stomach cramps and found Jack at Margaret's house.

He finished his drink and tossed the container into the plastic recycle bin.

"If you're going to be a NASCAR fan," Margaret told Amber, "you'd better learn to keep up with the action. After all, you wouldn't want to make a fool of yourself when some media type asks you a question about Johnny's performance, would you?"

Amber narrowed her eyes at her mother's rebuke, probably trying to figure out if the words held an intentional double meaning. "What are you doing here anyway?" she challenged irritably.

"I brought you something," Margaret said to Johnny. "Remember when we passed by your grandparents' house and I told you your grandmother loved to quilt?"

She retreated to the couch and picked up the large plastic bag on the floor beside it.

"I'd forgotten about this until I was cleaning out an old steamer trunk in the attic the other day." She removed a blue-and-green quilt, unfolded it and held it up for him to see. "Your grandmother made this."

Amber came closer and ran her fingers over the soft cotton. "Wow. This is really neat. All those little tiny stitches. It must have taken forever to sew. I'm sure I've never seen this before, Mom. Why didn't you ever bring it out?"

Margaret shrugged the question aside. "When you were little I put it away because I didn't want to take a chance on it getting messed up. Later…I guess I just forgot about it."

Johnny took it into his hands almost reverently. "These colors…" He studied it overall. "This design…"

"I think it's called an angel pattern. I'm sure there are dozens of variations, maybe hundreds. I've never quilted myself, so I'm no expert, but I don't imagine any two quilts are quite the same, since they're all handmade from scraps of fabric."

"Seems like I've seen this before."

"Maybe you have, since your grandmother made it. I thought you might like to have it."

"That's very kind of you," he said, his attention still fixed on the material in his hands. Finally he looked up. "You sure you don't want to keep it?"

"I'm happy to give it to you, Johnny. I'm sure your grandmother would want you to have it."

In a move that stunned Margaret and her daughter, Johnny leaned over and kissed the older woman gently on the cheek. "Thank you."

"You're welcome. Now—" she bustled to the door "—I've got to go. Traffic into town is going to be terrible."

BUT SHE DIDN'T GO to her car. With a backward glance she walked down the long line of motor homes, used the key she had been given when she'd had dinner with Jack earlier in the week, and let herself in.

The motor home amazed her. His accommodations on wheels cost several times more than her house and was far more lavishly appointed. She didn't have custom-made exotic wood cabinets or stainless steel appliances in her kitchen, and her counters weren't marble. As she walked across the living area toward the suede couch, she realized her carpet wasn't nearly as plush, either.

She didn't begrudge Jack the luxuries, any more than she did Johnny, whose motor home, brought over from Europe, was every bit as opulent. If she could afford such lavishness, she'd indulge, as well. Too bad everybody couldn't live this sumptuously.

Margaret knew it would be several hours before Jack showed up. Having won the race, he was in high demand by the media, his fans, team and sponsors.

She turned on the TV and channel surfed for everything she could find about the race, all the interviews with Jack, all the commentaries about his comeback. She also found a few editorial remarks about Johnny, mostly noting the Grand Prix driver hadn't done particularly well. They accepted his performance for what it was, rather lackluster; about what you'd expect from a rookie—or from a Grand Prix driver invading NASCAR territory. At least no one put him down. An hour later she turned off the TV, picked up the novel she'd brought with her and settled in to read.

Her eyelids were growing heavy when she heard the door open. Immediately she was alert, her pulse tripping. She sprang to her feet as Jack entered the RV.

His short, dark hair was a mess, sweat plastered to his head or standing up in discordant spikes where he'd probably run his fingers through it. His green-and-yellow uniform was tailored to his broad shoulders and narrow hips, but it looked as if it had been through a wringer. He smiled to her across the room, and her heartbeat accelerated.

"I was hoping you would stay with me after the race," he said, as he leaned against the counter and loosened one of his shoes.

"I didn't want to get in the way. It was your time," she said with an equal smile, her face unaccountably warm. She approached him almost shyly, intent on giving him a kiss.

"I wouldn't come any closer," he advised. "I reek. Give me a couple of minutes to clean up."

She chuckled rather than admit that even from several feet away he was sort of gamey. She was tempted to offer to scrub his back, but he'd already removed the other shoe, held them with the tips of his fingers and was moving toward the bedroom.

"Don't go away," he said, smiling over his shoulder.

She had no intention of leaving.

A minute later she heard the shower and in her mind's eye imagined him standing naked under its warm spray. The erotic image brought a pleasantly guilty tingling.

"He's probably starving," she muttered under her breath and admonished herself for not checking the refrigerator earlier to see what provisions he had. She did so now, found a six-pack of beer, a couple of bottles of white wine, yogurt, a dozen eggs, cheese, an unopened package of Braunschweiger, sealed packets of cold cuts for sandwiches, as well as fresh milk and orange juice. The crispers contained a variety of fruits and salad makings. His coach driver had obviously stocked up recently. She didn't bother inventorying in the freezer. She was confident of what she'd find there. Frozen dinners and pizza. This was definitely a bachelor pad.

Jack came out of the bedroom a few minutes later wearing a casual light blue shirt, its tail hanging out over baggy tan slacks. They didn't disguise the taut, athletic build beneath them. Well, they did, but she wasn't seeing the clothes. They didn't make the man.

His feet were bare, his dark, neatly trimmed hair in place now but still damp. Funny, she'd never noticed the subtle gray at the temples before. Quite distinguished looking, really.

"There's a party at the local watering hole," he said. "Care to go?"

"Thanks, but I'll stay here. You go ahead."

"Nah. I'm not much of a party animal, even when I win. I just thought I'd make the offer."

His eyes met hers, those clear blue depths that seemed to swallow her up. She shouldn't be feeling this…lust. But she was, and it felt so…dangerously good.

"You must be hungry."

He stepped close to her, wrapped his arms around her waist and pulled her up against him. "Only if you are."

Then he kissed her, an introductory meeting of lips followed by a genuine osculation, one that threatened to melt her sinews and curl her toes.

"I've been wanting to do that for hours, ever since the checkered flag," he said, still holding her against him. "Well, a lot longer than that actually."

She sighed against his chest, intoxicated by the clean smell of his skin and the firmness of his body. "The same thought has been going through my mind for some time now."

"Oh, really?" He kissed her again.

She definitely cooperated, but then she gently pushed him away. "How about you open one of those bottles of wine I noticed in the refrigerator, and I'll fix us an omelet with some of the cheese I saw in there."

"To be honest, I had a different kind of hunger in mind."

She knew exactly what he was referring to, but wasn't anticipation half the fun?

"Well," she drawled, "I think you have the makings of a Western omelet, if you prefer. My cooking's improved over the years. I can do things I never dreamed of doing before."

A grin narrowed his eyes. "Really? Well, I'm looking forward to that since you never...cooked for me back in high school."

"My mistake. They say the way to a man's heart—"

"You always had my heart, Megs."

The words thrilled and shamed her. Like Lillah, she'd squandered his gift, except Margaret had done it first. Remorse for her reckless insensitivity had her lowering her head.

He tipped her chin up and planted a kiss, soft and gentle this time, on her lips.

"I must say, though, your appetizers are wonderful," he added.

They set about preparing the impromptu meal. He was pouring them each a glass of wine when he asked, "Did you take him the quilt?"

She cracked half a dozen eggs into a metal bowl. "Yep. Told him I found it in the attic, had forgotten it was there."

He grated cheese. "What did he say?"

"He seemed genuinely touched to get it, kept staring at it, remarked how he thought it looked familiar. I told him since his grandmother made it he might very well have seen it before."

"Did he buy that?"

"I'm not sure."

The last time she and Jack had had dinner together he'd given her the quilt, one of the things Lillah had left behind when she ran out on him. It had been on Johnny's bed. Jack hoped it might trigger a flashback or two of him tucking the boy in for the night.

"Why didn't you just give it to him yourself?" Margaret asked. "It would have shown him you hadn't forgotten, that you cared."

Jack shook his head. "He would have thrown it in my face, accused me of trying to manipulate me." Which, he supposed, was what he was doing.

"Into remembering the daddy he loved and who loved him, who still loves him."

Jack didn't agree. "If that ever happens it'll have to come from inside him, Megs. I can provide the external stimulus, but I can't force it on him."

She knew he was right, but the process seemed to be taking so long, and it might never succeed. Margaret was convinced she'd made a serious mistake in not letting Johnny see his mother's diaries before she offered them to Jack. Lillah had left the decision about what to do with them to her discretion, as if she were endowed with some special wisdom and insight. Now, having given Jack the option, Margaret had no choice but to honor his request not to show them to his son, but she still hadn't been able to work up the courage to destroy them.

They finished their improvised meal, stacked the dishes in the dishwasher and took their wineglasses into the living room. Margaret sat on the couch. Jack sat beside her, close beside her, their legs touching. He threw his arm over the cushion behind her shoulders and pulled her against his chest.

"You sure you don't need to go to that party?" she asked. "I mean, you were the winner today."

"I'm where I want to be."

She smiled up at him. "You're where I want you to be, too."

He bent down and kissed her on the lips. "Actually, there is another place I'd prefer to be right now."

She had to grin. "And where might that be?"

"In the other room. There's a piece of furniture there I'd like to share with you, see if it's comfortable enough for two."

Her eyes sparkled. "Let's go find out then."

She climbed to her feet, extending her hand to his. They stood there and kissed again, then she led him by the hand to his bedroom.

CHAPTER ELEVEN

IT WAS AFTER EIGHT O'CLOCK the following morning when Margaret stepped out the door of Jack's motor home. She'd intended to leave much earlier, but when he invited her to share his shower—to save hot water, of course—temptation overruled good sense. After all, she'd told herself, acceding to Jack's suggestion would only delay her departure by a few minutes.

She smiled to herself. It wasn't fair to blame it on him. She'd been a very willing participant in their adventures the night before and this morning. She'd almost forgotten how much she missed sex. She'd certainly never experienced it the way she had with Jack. Gary had been good. She had no complaints or regrets in that regard, but with Jack... Well, with him it was all new and exciting again. He'd taken physical intimacy to another level, another plane. Or maybe planet.

"Mom?"

Margaret froze and the grin she suspected she'd been wearing slipped into alarm as she instinctively turned around to face the familiar voice.

"Amber!" With her heart suddenly pounding to a different drummer, she demanded, "What are you doing here?"

"I could ask you the same thing." Amber had her hands behind her back as she bounced on the balls of her feet and surveyed the motor home from which Margaret had just emerged. The springing motion ceased as awareness dawned.

"I thought you and Johnny were leaving this morning for California."

"We are, but there were things he had to do with a sponsor or an agent or somebody first." With pinched brow Amber studied her mother disapprovingly. "I thought you left yesterday."

"I was going to, but I changed my mind."

"Obviously." The word dripped with sarcasm. "This is Jack Dolman's motor home, isn't it?" More a statement than a question.

Margaret fumed at herself. She should have been more careful, more discreet. If she'd left an hour ago as she'd planned she wouldn't be in this embarrassing position now.

Before she could answer or come up with a question of her own to change the subject, Amber said, "You're wearing the same clothes you were wearing yesterday." Her eyes went wide as the full implication of what she'd said penetrated. "You were here…. You spent the night with him, didn't you?"

Margaret wanted to tell her it was none of her business. The mortification of having to answer to her own daughter for her nocturnal activities was so weird it numbed her brain and words never reached her vocal cords.

"I can't believe it." Her daughter let out a mocking

laugh. "My perfect mother, shacking up with a race car driver."

Heat rose to Margaret's face. Deciding it was time to take control of the situation and recalling that the best defense was a good offense, Margaret asked, "What are you doing out this early in the morning?"

"I told you," her daughter responded, still reveling in the chink she'd found in her mother's moral armor, "Johnny had things to take care of before we leave."

"That explains his being out at this hour, but not you."

"Oh, for crying out loud." Amber scowled at her mother.

"You've never been a morning person," Margaret persisted.

"Give me a break, Mother. Can't I even go out for a cup of coffee and a doughnut without being accused of a crime?"

Crime? Who said anything about a crime?

Even as she was thinking the words Margaret noticed her daughter's slightly bloodshot eyes. She'd so hoped Johnny's suspicions the afternoon before had been mistaken, that Amber hadn't succumbed to the lure of narcotics. "You haven't been buying drugs, have you?"

"What?" When Margaret didn't immediately answer, Amber shouted, "You're just like Johnny, always picking on me. You never give me a chance."

"Chance for what, Amber? I'm concerned about you. Johnny is, too. You heard what he said. If you get caught doing drugs you're on your own. He can't protect you, and he can't afford to be associated with an addict."

"Does caffeine count, dammit?"

Amber produced a grease-stained white paper bag with a coffee company logo on it from behind her back and hurled it toward the motor home. It hit one of the tires and splattered steaming coffee. She glared at her mother and strode down the walkway toward Johnny's place.

She's on something, Margaret thought. She never used to have these temper tantrums, these overreactions. Her heart sank. What was she going to do? Amber was over eighteen now, no longer a minor. She was fully responsible under the law for her actions and able to make her own decisions.

Margaret broke into a jog to catch up.

"Oh, honey. I'm sorry. I'm just so worried about you. I love you so much. I hate to see you do this to yourself."

The plea only seemed to incense the girl more.

"Do what, Mom? I'm not doing anything. Just leave me alone, okay? Leave me the hell alone."

She broke into a run between the rows of luxury motor homes toward Johnny's.

Feeling guilty and defeated, Margaret watched her daughter's back as she fled from her. Hearing fresh footsteps behind her, she turned and saw Jack approaching. He was casually dressed in chinos and a green-and-yellow knit shirt. Without saying a word he came up beside her and extended his arm across her back. His touch was so reassuring she found herself instinctively leaning into his side and resting her head against his shoulder.

"I don't know what to do," she murmured. "I don't know where I've gone wrong or how I can make it right again."

He squeezed her tenderly. "Maybe you haven't done

anything wrong, Megs, and maybe there isn't anything you can do to make it right."

She twisted enough to look up at him. "Don't say that, Jack. Please. I'm her mother. I brought her up. There must be something I can do. I can't just stand by and watch her destroy herself."

"There comes a point when children have to make their own decisions. We can't always make them do what we want them to."

He was thinking of Johnny, but that situation was different. Johnny had been under the influence of his mother and Antonio, people who had authority over him and who calculatingly lied to him. It wasn't the same with Amber, but of course Jack didn't see it that way. All he saw was his own inability to make the mother of his child love him, and in failing to do that he had lost the love of the son, as well.

"She seemed pretty upset about finding you here," he said.

"It's not as if she doesn't know about the birds and the bees."

He chuckled softly. "That applies to other people's parents, never our own." He linked his arm with hers and turned them around. "No need for you to run off now. The cat is out of the bag. Come on back for a second cup of coffee and we'll talk."

Back in the motor home, with cups refilled, they sat side by side at the counter.

"You know how much I care about you, Megs. You've awakened in me a world I thought was lost. But pleasure can't be allowed to change our priorities. Nothing is more important than family. If what we have is going to come between you and your daughter, maybe we should cool it, at least for a while, until things settle down."

She fingered the handle of her cup, gazing at its contents blindly. "Is that what you want, Jack? To cool it?"

He swiveled toward her, took her hand, felt its softness and warmth. "No, but if—"

"Neither do I," she declared, not giving him a chance to finish. "Last night…" She paused. "I don't want to cool it, either."

THE CAT WAS OUT OF THE BAG in Johnny's motor home, as well.

He had just returned from a meeting with Mac Roberts. He'd expected their discussion to be about his lackluster showing in the opening race. The team owner, Vaughn Steiner, had expressed satisfaction with Johnny's performance, but he suspected his crew chief would be less patronizing. Johnny was prepared to fly out to Los Angeles that afternoon, so he could get a head start on the other drivers coming in Thursday. He'd walk the course, studying it. Every racetrack was unique. Each had its own quirks and idiosyncrasies. Johnny had already visited the track outside Fontana, California on his tour during the holidays, but a second visit before the race couldn't hurt. He'd have to rearrange a couple of guest appearances, but the schedule was manageable.

The meeting wasn't about the last race or the upcoming one, however. It was about Amber. Mac wanted Johnny to ditch her.

"She's trouble, Johnny," the older man said with

fatherly concern. "She's been floating around the infield like the tooth fairy, when she isn't getting into people's faces."

"What are you talking about?"

"She walked through the concessions area yesterday and gave one of the vendors a boatload of trouble, claiming he had the colors wrong on a souvenir car. Turns out she got the numbers reversed. The colors were correct."

"Damn."

"She apologized profusely when one of the other vendors pointed out the discrepancy and nothing more came of it. Fortunately there wasn't any media around. I don't have to tell you what can happen to your career if she gets caught with drugs on her."

"I'm clean," Johnny insisted, "any test will prove that."

"Legally maybe—"

"Not maybe, Mac. I don't use."

"Doesn't make any difference. You have an image to maintain, and rumors, even if they're not true, can do fatal damage. You know as well as I do you can't prove a negative. An accusation by anyone, especially a girl-friend, could put an end to your career in NASCAR before it really gets started."

"She'd never do that."

"Druggies will do anything, son. They act like cornered rats when they're challenged."

Johnny felt his pulse rise. He didn't like being called *son* as though he were an adolescent, and he didn't ap-preciate having his girlfriend compared to vermin. His jaw tightened.

As if reading his thoughts, the crew chief said, "Look, Johnny, I'm really not trying to tick you off. All I'm saying is what I think has to be said, for your own good, and for everybody else's on your team, because if you go down, we go down with you. You don't want that, and neither do I."

He paused, observed Johnny with a measuring eye, then pressed on.

"Amber is a very pretty girl, and I suspect reasonably intelligent, but she's making bad choices, decisions that could have a very negative impact on all of us. Either set her straight, make sure she stays clean, or drop her before it's too late."

Johnny left a minute later, his teeth aching from keeping them clenched. As much as he resented the advice, he also knew it was both well intended and needed to be taken seriously.

He returned to his motor home to find Amber already sprawled out on the couch, TV controller in hand, flicking through channels.

"I'm glad you're here," he said. "We need to talk."

"You won't believe who I just ran into and where," she said, tossing aside the remote and sitting up, unaware of the tenseness in his demeanor. "I caught Mom coming out of Jack Dolman's place. She spent the night with him."

That brought him up short. "Are you sure?" He noticed she was jumpy, fidgety.

"Yes, I'm sure," she retorted with irritation, as if his question had been a personal insult, an attack on her honesty and integrity. She went over to one of the stools, pulled it out, then shoved it back under the counter. "Johnny, I caught her coming out of Jack's motor home, wearing the same clothes she was wearing yesterday. What does that tell you? And her hair was still damp from a shower."

"So she spent the night with him," he muttered, as if it were of no significance.

"Don't you understand?" Amber lifted her shoulders dramatically and let them fall. "My mother is sleeping with your father."

He exploded into nervous laughter. "Don't worry, *cara*. That doesn't make us brother and sister."

She didn't think it was funny. "It doesn't bother you?"

More than he wanted to admit. He'd understood even before they returned to the States from Italy that Margaret had once been Jack's girlfriend, that she'd thrown him over for Amber's father. She was a widow now and still an attractive woman. If she had any lingering affection for the man she'd rejected—and she obviously did—why shouldn't she explore it?

"They're both adults," he reminded Amber. "She used to be his girlfriend in high school, remember? Before he started going with my mother. What's the big deal?"

"She's sleeping with the enemy. That's what's the big deal."

He'd trusted Margaret, thought of her as a friend. He still did. A friend but not an ally. Was that possible? Was she spying on him for his father? He seriously doubted it. What could she possibly learn from him or from Amber that would help Jack in any way?

Her goal was undoubtedly to bring the two men

together, and maybe it was Jack's, as well, but the bond between father and son had been broken a long time ago. It was beyond mending now.

"I'm more concerned about you," Johnny stated.

Amber wrinkled her brows as she regarded him suspiciously. "Me?" She spun around. "There's nothing wrong with me."

"You're high as a kite, Amber."

She put her hands on her hips. "I am not."

"If I asked you to take a drug test right now, you'd fail."

She stomped across the room, plopped down in an armchair, climbed immediately back onto her feet, made a small circle in the middle of the carpet, then faced him again.

"Why don't you then?" she demanded. "You're just looking for an excuse to dump me."

"*Cara... Bellissima,* don't you understand? I'm looking for a reason not to. I can't figure out why you do this to yourself. You don't need to. I like you the way you are without all that junk in you."

She turned away, but she couldn't stand still. She pranced around the room and finally settled onto the couch, legs extended.

"I don't know why I care about you, *cara,*" he said, "but I do. Keep this up, though, and I'll have to let you go."

She stormed and raged. Accused him of not really caring for her. She calmed, kissed him, swore her undying love, then went on the attack again. He was just using her....

He let her rant. The motor home was well insulated; even someone standing directly outside the door wouldn't be able to hear what was going on, not distinctly, anyway. He also knew in her present state there wasn't much chance of stopping her, short of violence, and he would never hurt a woman. Jack had abused his mother, and she'd apparently endured it until Antonio came along, but Johnny would never strike a woman.

Later, after whatever Amber was on had worn off and she'd rested up, he'd try talking sense into her. This had happened before, and she'd always insisted she wasn't taking any narcotics. She'd be fine for several weeks after that, then something would trigger another episode. Maybe, he thought, if he talked to Margaret, together they'd be able to figure out what her problem was.

CHAPTER TWELVE

In sunny California Jack started out in the eighth position and ended up finishing sixteenth after he blew a tire in the backstretch in the ninety-seventh lap. Johnny did much better, starting out seventeenth and finishing tenth.

He had the smug expression wiped off his face in Vegas, however, where he almost won the pole position, nailed the number two slot, but limped under the checkered flag in thirty-seventh place. He'd been working the front of the pack until the twenty-fourth lap when the unique banking of the Vegas track caused him to lose downward pressure on his spoiler, set his tail to floating and, before he was able to reestablish control, hurled him against the wall.

To his credit he was able to recover, but then forty-two laps later Jem Nordstrom drove up on his tail coming out of Turn Two, established a few second's draft, bumped him and sent him flying into the wall again.

This time on the rebound Johnny slammed into three other cars, skidded across the track, clipped another car and rolled twice. A quick check confirmed he was unhurt and that the car was structurally and mechanically sound, so he was able to get back on the track and run the final laps for points, but by then all hope of recapturing his earlier position was a faded memory.

His mood when he climbed out of the crumpled vehicle reflected it. Fortunately no cameras or microphones were around, and the expletives he was rattling off were in Italian. His team, unfamiliar with the foreign language, simply smiled at the melodious sounds he was making.

Much later that afternoon Vaughn Steiner called a meeting in the hauler to review the race with him and Mac Roberts.

"Nordstrom did that intentionally," Johnny complained, when they came to that taped portion of the race.

Steiner and Roberts traded glances, first in bewilderment, then with amusement.

"Of course he did," Mac replied in a tone that came close to a snicker. "What did you expect him to do when you were just sitting there in his path, asking for it?"

Johnny was taken aback by the sarcasm.

"I warned you about Nordstrom," Steiner added.

"In Grand Prix—"

Steiner raised his hand. "Stop right there, Johnny. This is stock car racing, not Grand Prix. The gentlemanly conventions of Formula 1 don't apply here. If you want to succeed in this game you're going to have to change your mind-set. The rules are different in NASCAR. We can do things in stock cars you can't do in open-wheel—"

"Like touch each other without wiping both of you out," the crew chief contributed.

There was a reason Formula 1 was called open-wheel racing. The most exposed parts of Formula 1 vehicles were the four wheels, which meant coming in contact with another object, be it a barrier, a wall or another moving vehicle, just about guaranteed serious problems, loss of control and incapacitating damage.

Grand Prix driving etiquette, therefore, centered on establishing and maintaining distance from other vehicles, not proximity, and because Grand Prix tracks were road courses with plenty of twists and turns, drivers had few opportunities to safely pass each other.

The things that were paramount in open-wheel racing, consequently, were winning the pole and working out a strategy for pit stops. It wasn't unusual for the order of cars crossing the finish line to be very close to their starting positions, all of which was much different from NASCAR racing where cars moved in tight packs, touching each other didn't necessarily bode disaster and one's position in the pack could and often did change dramatically a dozen or more times in the course of an afternoon.

Mac grabbed a cold drink from the refrigerator and resumed his place on one of the vinyl benches while Steiner rewound to the part where Johnny had been nailed by Nordstrom. He and Roberts pointed out a host of things going on around Johnny at the time, many of which Johnny had ignored or been unaware of.

"How was I supposed to know that?" Johnny demanded in frustration, when Steiner commented on Nordstrom shifting lanes two rows behind him only seconds before getting into position to deliver the bump that sent Johnny careening into the wall. "He wasn't in my field of vision."

"You have to anticipate other drivers' moves," Steiner replied, "and trust your spotter to keep you informed of what's going on around you. Brad is a good spotter. He knows who to watch, what to look for and what to pass on."

"He told you Jem was moving up," Mac added sharply.

Johnny shot his crew chief a startled glance.

"I checked the audio tape," Mac explained, "to make sure my memory wasn't playing tricks on me. He told you Nordstrom and O'Bryan were drafting in your right rear quadrant."

Johnny's brow furrowed. "I was focusing on Dolman. He was directly behind me. He'd been dogging me—"

"As a result of concentrating on one driver you lost track of the real challenger," Steiner said. "Nordstrom is one of the most aggressive drivers out there. He's good, not just because he knows how to handle the wheel, but because he thinks ahead."

Johnny had screwed up. They all knew it, but only he knew why.

MARGARET DEBATED Jack's invitation to follow him on the NASCAR circuit. Not that she didn't enjoy the races—or his company—but she'd checked into the local hospice organization and been provisionally accepted as a visiting nurse. It would be only part-time during the initial period, essentially on-the-job orientation to see if she was suited to the work and really wanted to do it. As eager as she was to get started, she demurred.

Spending time with Jack was definitely appealing, but the bigger issue, the concern that convinced her to go with him, was Amber. Margaret was worried about her daughter. Something was wrong; she didn't know what, and every attempt to elicit information from her resulted in the young woman's denial that there even was a problem.

How times had changed. She didn't consider herself a prude, but her upbringing had been fairly straitlaced. No underage drinking, no premarital sex and definitely no drugs. Now she was, as Amber had phrased it, shacking up, or at least considering shacking up, with Jack Dolman, while her nineteen-year-old daughter was doing the same with Jack's estranged son.

It wasn't that Margaret didn't trust Johnny to treat her right. The Italian Grand Prize, as one pundit had crowned him, might have received a terrible example from his adoptive father, but Johnny wasn't a predator. Margaret wasn't worried about him hurting Amber or allowing anyone else to. The problem, as Margaret saw it, was that he wasn't with her most of the time, nor was she his primary responsibility. But she was Margaret's, and though Margaret couldn't babysit her daughter 24/7, she could stay close at hand, keep an eye on her and be available if she was needed.

Margaret drove down to the Atlanta racetrack on Thursday before the race and located Jack's motor home in the drivers and owners section of the infield late that afternoon. Predictably he wasn't there. No matter. Right now she had a more important mission to perform.

After freshening up, she left the motor home, ensuring the door was securely locked behind her, and set off in search of Johnny's place. Finding it one row over and four rows down, she knocked and waited.

She was surprised when he opened the door a minute later. She'd expected Amber.

"She went shopping with Mac's wife," he explained, after ushering her in and bestowing a kiss on her right cheek, then her left in European fashion. "I'm glad you're here. We need to talk."

"I agree."

He invited her to sit on the couch. He took the love seat.

"You staying with Jack Dolman?" His tone was polite but clearly disapproving.

"I have a hotel suite in town," she said. "In fact, that's one of the reasons I'm looking for Amber, to give her a key in case she wants to come by."

His eyes, so startlingly like Jack's, were the identical blue color, and held the same intensity. "But you won't be there."

"I may or may not." Matching his veiled hostility, she asked, "Is that your concern?"

"I don't think it's wise," he stated.

"And I don't recall asking your opinion or advice," she retorted. "He's a good man, Johnny. I know you don't believe that, but if you'd give him a chance you'd find out for yourself."

"You may think so, but can you be sure?"

His stiff-necked attitude irritated her. She was

tempted to tell him he'd been duped. If he'd just open his eyes—and his heart—he'd see that. But Jack was right. His son simply wasn't ready yet.

"I know what you've been told about him, Johnny," she said after a pause, "but it's not true."

"I wouldn't want you to get hurt."

Frustration screamed through her. It was as though he hadn't heard anything she'd said, and yet, despite his patronizing tone, she didn't doubt the sincerity of his statement.

"Jack isn't going to hurt me," she insisted.

"I don't think you should be staying with him."

The irony of the conversation wasn't lost on Margaret. Here she was being asked to justify her relationship with a man she'd known since high school to the nearly thirty-year-old international playboy who was sleeping with her teenage daughter.

Praying for patience and wisdom, she closed her eyes, but only for a moment.

"I appreciate your concern, but I know Jack Dolman a lot better than you do, and I can assure you what you've been told about him is incorrect and your judgment of him wholly unfair." In the frigid silence that followed, she added, "If at any time you want to discuss what you think you know about him, I'll be glad to oblige. Until you're willing to listen, however, there's not much point in my wasting my breath."

His jaw shifted.

"Let's talk about Amber."

He exhaled, relieved at the change of subject. "Yes, let's. She's different lately." He crossed one leg over the other and draped one arm along the back of the seat. "She's changed since she's come home. Why?"

"I was hoping you could tell me. You accused her of taking drugs. Is she?"

"I don't know."

"Would you tell me if you did?"

He seemed both surprised and offended by the question. "I'm sorry you have to ask that, Margaret. You and I may not see eye to eye on Jack Dolman, but don't for a minute think I don't care about Amber. I would never do anything to hurt her, and I certainly don't want to see her hurt herself."

"So you've seen no evidence of her using drugs?"

"Aside from the mood swings, no. No needle marks, for instance."

"Have you been able to discern any pattern to when she has these mood swings?"

He shook his head and brought his upraised arm back to his side.

"Not really. She's fine for a while, then she has what I call one of her crazy days. Sometimes she's giddy and silly. Other times she's hyper. It lasts maybe a day or so and then she's back to being her old self."

His experience pretty much matched Margaret's. "Have you seen her take anything…or found anything? Pills, tablets, crystals?"

"Never," he replied. "Well, once. She was complaining of having a headache, so I gave her a couple of aspirin. Seemed to do the trick. An hour or so later she was fine. But I gave her tablets out of *my* bottle."

"Something's going on," Margaret muttered, downcast, staring into space. "I wish I could figure out what it is. She's never had a problem with drugs or alcohol," she assured him. "This doesn't make any sense." She got up from her seat and moped to the door. "If you think of something or find anything, will you call me?"

"Of course." He had risen with her and trailed behind her to the door. "And if you discover anything... Margaret, I really want to help any way I can. I care for her more than you know."

She turned and studied him a moment. "Thank you." She put her hand on the doorknob. "Tell Amber to call me on my cell if she wants to get together for dinner or just hang out. Otherwise I'll see her tomorrow."

"I will."

She opened the door and stepped outside. "Good luck qualifying tomorrow. I hope you get the pole."

JOHNNY DIDN'T GET the pole the next day. He took fourth place and on Sunday again held his own, that is, he finished fourth. His owner and crew chief seemed happy with the result, and in Grand Prix it would have been respected, but Johnny wasn't content. This was NASCAR, he reminded himself. The objective was to maneuver and win.

Bristol, which followed, was another matter altogether, a complete contrast to any challenge he'd come up against in Formula 1 or even NASCAR. Grand Prix courses varied in length from about two and a half to nearly six miles. Bristol was the shortest track on the NASCAR circuit: half a mile. The five-hundred-mile race encompassed a thousand laps, each lasting less than twenty seconds. It was dizzying for the driver.

Johnny started in seventh position but ended in fifteenth. With nerves tingling and head still spinning he wound his way out the window of his black-and-silver car. Laughing at his obvious light-headedness, Vaughn Steiner and Mac Roberts assured him he'd done well.

In the races that followed, Martinsville, Texas, Phoenix, Talladega, Johnny continued to make good showings, always coming in among the top ten. He didn't win any races, but with each competition he was moving up and feeling more confident. He was also racking up significant points toward the Chase for the NASCAR NEXTEL Cup. Both the media and the racing world were beginning to take notice.

Jack Dolman was doing well, too. He won twice, at Darlington and Pocono, but he also had a few unlucky breaks. He was eliminated in Richmond because of a pileup that destroyed his car—he walked away without a scratch. His engine blew there, also. Pointwise, however, he and Johnny were a statistical tie.

"You've won so many races on the Formula 1 circuit in Europe and Asia. Did you expect to be doing so well at NASCAR here in the States, too?" a television sportscaster asked Johnny after he came in second in the first of three races in Charlotte.

"I'm pleased and excited by it all," he responded. "The reception I've received from the NASCAR community and the fans has been unbelievable."

"So you're not surprised by your good showing?" the reporter persisted.

He refused to fall for the *gotcha* question. If he said he was surprised he came across as lacking in confidence. If he said he wasn't, the impression drawn would be that he was arrogant and full of himself.

"Every race brings its own challenges," he said with a good-natured chuckle. "And every result is something of a shock. It's the unpredictability of the sport that makes it so exciting for driver and spectator alike."

It wasn't until the last of the three back-to-back races in Charlotte, however, that the media began to link the names of Jack Dolman and Johnny Rendisi as the primary contenders for the season's championship.

"Johnny, you and Jack Dolman have been trading number one positions for the last five races. Even now you're only ten points apart. Your closest competitor is fifty points behind you. Do you think you're going to win at the end of the season?"

"Time will tell, won't it?" He flashed his best, most confident smile, knowing the camera was focused on him. "I can tell you this. I'm going to be giving it my best shot, and I expect Dolman will, too."

"He's going to win. I know he is," Amber told the reporter. She had her arm around Johnny's waist. "He's the best."

THE RESPONSES the media received from Jack to similar questions were equally diplomatic, except that once he slipped and called Johnny "the kid." The reporter reminded him Rendisi was almost thirty years old and already a world-class racing champion.

"I plead seniority," Jack quipped, "in years and experience in NASCAR. He's young enough to be my son." He wondered how "the kid" would react to that when he saw it on TV.

"But there's also no denying Johnny's good," Jack continued. "Not too many drivers make a successful crossover from open-wheel racing to stock cars and do well in both. Looks like Johnny's one of that rare breed."

No one seemed to notice that Dolman never referred to Rendisi by his last name. It was always Johnny.

"So you think he has a chance at the Cup?"

Jack laughed. "I sure hope so. Isn't that what we're racing for?"

"You wouldn't be…upset, even offended by being beat by a rookie who's never driven a stock car before this season?"

"Like I said," Jack replied with a grin, "we're all in this to win, and of course someone will. I just hope it's me. I'm going to do everything in my power to come out on top, but we'll have to wait till the very last lap of the very last race to find out."

Interviews with owners and crew chiefs for both teams yielded similar reactions—cautious confidence that their man was going to prevail.

Amber was interviewed on her own several times and came off, in Margaret's estimation, like something of an airhead, bubbly and excited, and not particularly smart. It broke Margaret's heart.

MARGARET DIDN'T SAY anything to Jack or Amber about her conversation with Johnny in Atlanta. Since then Johnny had continued to be polite and well mannered. She doubted an outsider would notice any difference in their attitudes toward one another. Even Amber seemed unaware of a growing distance between them.

The situation had Margaret doing a lot of thinking—or rather rethinking.

Johnny was convinced his father was the villain in his life and seemed determined to shut out any arguments to the contrary. The diaries might change his mind, but would they? His mother had already told him Antonio's version of events was false, and he'd refused to listen.

Margaret had to agree with Jack's assessment that Johnny wouldn't thank her for destroying his illusions about Lillah and Antonio. But this wasn't about Margaret. Any hope of Johnny altering his opinion of Jack would have to arise from Johnny seeing a quality in his father that contradicted the stories he'd been told. Again she considered the diaries. They were proof, written in Lillah's own hand over a period of more than twenty years that Jack had acted honorably. They revealed her slow awakening to her own selfishness and gullibility, her growing awareness of her second husband's deceptiveness and dishonesty, and finally her acceptance of blame for what she'd done to both her son and his father.

But if Margaret turned the diaries over to Johnny now, she wasn't sure he'd read them—or read them accurately. Prejudice had a way of distorting truth.

Which left her in a quandary. She wanted desperately for Jack to get his son back, and she was sure she had the means to effect that—except Jack had forbidden her to use it. Maybe forbid was too strong a word. He didn't have the power to forbid her from doing anything, but she agreed not to show them to his son. Passing them on to Johnny now might or might not change the young man's attitude toward his father. For sure, though, it would turn Jack against her for violating his trust in her.

She wondered what had possessed her to leave him all those years ago. No, she didn't wonder. She knew. Jealousy. She'd been jealous of his love of racing. He'd loved cars, it seemed to her back then, more than he'd loved her. In a way it had probably been true. He'd certainly taken her more for granted than he had them. They constantly needed tuning and adjusting, continuous attention, whereas she... He assumed she'd always be there for him. Dependable. Faithful.

But a girl didn't want to be taken for granted, like a wrench or screwdriver. She wanted to be coddled, cooed over, treasured and worried about.

So she'd tried to make *him* jealous.

Gary Truesdale, the transfer student, came along. He was handsome, too, talented and gregarious. Jack never dedicated a race to Margaret, but Gary dedicated songs to her. Jack never told her she inspired him to win races, but Gary said she inspired him to blow his horn better, to express his music in a way that was distinctively hers.

At least that was what he'd claimed.

She learned later he was better at playing games than she was, but by then it was too late. What she'd failed to realize back then was that Jack didn't play games. Not that kind, at least. Not with people's emotions.

When she told him she'd found someone else, he believed her. She'd expected him to fight for her, but the only kind of competition he understood was on four wheels.

He told her he'd miss her—a lot—but he respected her right to make her own decisions, to choose the people she wanted to be with. He even added that he was sorry he hadn't lived up to her expectations, though he also admitted he didn't know precisely what those expectations were. He was grateful for the time they'd had together. Then he wished her happiness.

Still she hadn't been smart enough to recognize he was simple—in the good sense—and she was being stupid.

Then Lillah moved in and the tables were reversed. Margaret now had to fight for Jack, but when Lillah announced she was pregnant, the game was over, and Margaret knew she'd lost Jack for good.

Who would have thought they'd find each other again after thirty years, thanks to Lillah?

After Pocono, Margaret returned home and continued cleaning out the house on Oakmore Street. The repairs and renovations she'd ordered were complete. All that was left now was to get it painted and put it on the market.

She tackled the attic. It wasn't very large, but it was cluttered with the accumulation of twenty years of frugal living. Frugality aside, she wondered why she'd saved most of it.

Then she came across the box of Amber's CDs. The rock collection was downstairs. These CDs were different. Plenty of jazz. A few pop. Some country fiddling. But mostly classical music featuring the violin. The three Bs. Bach, Beethoven, Brahms. Other romantics. Tchaikovsky, Sibelius, Schubert, Debussy.

She missed hearing their warm, melodious, intricate harmonies, the long musical puzzles that were finally resolved in climactic celebrations of triumph.

She pushed another box aside and found it, the black leather violin case. The outside was battered and scarred. The instrument hadn't been new when they'd bought it ten years ago, and would never be mistaken for a Stradivarius, but it could be made to sing. Margaret opened the clasp.

Inside lay the shiny instrument on its fitted green felt form. Impulsively she plucked a string. Loose. But even the flat, sour twang conjured up an image, and for no apparent reason Margaret felt tears burn her eyes.

Why Amber chose to take up the violin was a mystery. Gary played the trumpet. His combo members played a variety of other instruments. Piano, sax, clarinet, bass, drums, on occasion even the xylophone. Nobody played the fiddle. Even the bass player only strummed his stringed giant.

But somewhere around the age of eight Amber fell in love with the violin, asked to take lessons, attended them faithfully and practiced without being told.

Then her father died, and she packed up her CDs and her fiddle, carted them up to the attic and abandoned them.

Margaret closed the case and took it downstairs along with the box of CDs and put them in Amber's room. It would be up to her to decide what she wanted to do with them. Keep them or sell them. She hoped her daughter would keep them, but given Amber's current attitude, Margaret's expectations weren't high.

CHAPTER THIRTEEN

THE BUILDUP TO THE RACE in Sonoma was more intense than usual. Since this track was not the conventional oval but an irregular road course in California's famous wine country with twelve twists and turns, as well as dips and hills, it most resembled a European Grand Prix contest.

"Remember, you're racing on his turf," Cal said, as Jack put on his helmet.

"But in my cars," Jack shot back.

They'd had this conversation before, and Jack was getting tired of hearing his son was a shoo-in for this race. He couldn't completely blame Cal. The media gurus were saying the same thing, that a Formula 1 driver had a natural advantage on a road-type course.

Jack's adrenaline was pumping, as it always did before a race. He was leading his son in points, but not by much. The boy—the man—had been giving him far more competition than either Jack or Cal had expected. If Johnny beat his father in this race it could put him substantially ahead, and Jack wasn't quite ready for the sneering gloat the kid would give him.

Jack slithered through the window opening of the Number 424 car, secured the five-point harness that kept him snug in the customized seat, attached the steering wheel, did an audio check into his mouthpiece and listened to the response in his headset. He confirmed his reception, reached forward and flipped the toggle switch to start the engine.

The 750-horsepower V-8 growled to life. The deafening roar as he revved it was muffled by his helmet, but the vibrations it produced radiated from his tailbone up his spine clear to his earlobes.

He checked the gauges on the panel. All the needles were where they should be. In this world of speed and intimidation anything that could go wrong eventually did, so he never took mechanical performance for granted. The biggest threat, of course, came from the human element.

He ran a series of pace laps to warm up his engine and get his butt adjusted to the feel of the road, then he settled into the physical routine of driving while he fine-tuned his mental attitude.

He'd never won a race at this track. Never done very well here, for that matter. His best showing had been seventh, and that was only because on that particular occasion five cars had wiped out ahead of him on Turn Eleven, the hard switchback at the southeast corner of the irregular course. There was no question Johnny had the advantage here. He was, after all, a recognized champion in road course racing, so there would certainly be no disgrace on Jack's part if the younger man trounced him. But pride wouldn't let even his son defeat him without a fight.

The call went out. They lined up. Johnny had taken

the pole. Jack was in ninth position. Not all that great, but not bad, either. On a standard oval it gave him a fighting chance. On this irregular course, far less of one. Which meant he would have to be aggressive from the outset, not bide his time as he sometimes did on other tracks.

His competitors gunned their engines. He did, too. The combined rumble of thousands of horsepower had the world around him vibrating, rattling his bones, quivering his muscles. And sent his adrenaline pumping.

The green flag. Go. Go. Go. Go. Go.

It occurred to Jack after the third lap that he wasn't alone in his discomfort with this type of race. Watkins Glen didn't fit the standard oval or D-shaped pattern, either, but it wasn't as radical as this course, where everyone seemed to be a rookie. Except for one driver.

Johnny held the lead for thirteen laps, dogged all the way by Rafael O'Bryan. Then something happened—Jack's spotter hadn't seen what—and O'Bryan was out in front.

Six laps later Jack had moved forward another two positions. He damn near wiped out on the infamous Turn Eleven, but managed to hold his ground. There was definitely less jockeying for position in this race than in its predecessors.

What followed were the things that made a race interesting and kept the fans coming back for more.

Spinouts, collisions, blown tires, blown engines. Cars cartwheeled, tumbled, sent off cascades of sparks, burst into flames and emitted little mushroom clouds of black-and-white stench-filled smoke. Fire crews were kept busy, as well as ambulances. But the safety features designed and implemented over fifty years of experience all worked. Drivers walked away from burning cars and mangled wrecks to race another day.

The crowds went wild.

Midway through the race the yellow flag went up when a failed car produced an oil slick halfway through Turn Seven. Almost twenty minutes were lost cleaning it up. Half the field, including Jack and Johnny, decided to take a pit stop, adding to the traffic congestion on pit road.

By the three-quarters point, forty-three cars had been reduced to thirty-four.

Johnny was once more in the lead.

Jack had moved up to fifth place.

Rafael O'Bryan was directly in front of him. Jem Nordstrom behind him. Jack knew the guy riding his tail was the bigger threat. Nordstrom was a predator. A quick draft, followed by even a light tap at the approach to a turn, especially one as sharp as seven or eleven could have him doing flat windmills across the roadway while the rest of the pack streamed by.

They played zigzag for most of the next sixteen laps, then, suddenly Nordstrom careened to the right and was out of the picture.

"What the hell happened?" he asked into his mouthpiece.

"Finnegan Jarvis took him out," his spotter explained with a hint of glee in his voice.

Jack had no doubt it had been planned. In public and to the media, Jarvis always had the nicest things to say about his old buddy, Nordstrom. The two had started out together on the same team. Nordstrom had done well. Jarvis had been forced back to the Busch Series for three years, and had only reappeared in the NASCAR NEXTEL Series this season. This was the third time he'd wiped out his former teammate.

"Nordstrom going to be back?" Jack asked.

There was a long pause. "Judging from the fire, I don't think so."

"He did get out, didn't he?"

"He's fine," the spotter immediately replied. No one laughed or joked about fire or wished it—or any other injury—on their worst enemy. "Got out before it erupted."

"What's the count?"

"Twelve laps to go. Down to twenty-nine cars, eight of you in the lead pack. Rendisi still in front."

"Offer OB a draft."

Fifteen seconds later Jack was an inch away from O'Bryan's bumper. Together they passed the third car, then the second. Jack wasn't surprised when O'Bryan shimmied to the right, then the left, breaking the draft. Jack would have done the same a little sooner than Rafael had.

It was Johnny, Rafe, Jack, in that order, for the next six laps.

Johnny was on the inside. O'Bryan rode his tailpipe, forcing him to maneuver right to avoid a draft and the inevitable bump that would send him flying out of control. O'Bryan didn't follow, preferring to hold the inside, hoping Johnny would steer far enough to the right to allow O'Bryan to slip in beside him. Johnny didn't. They held their positions, O'Bryan fixed to Johnny's left quarter for another two laps.

Jack saw his chance. They were diagonally crossing the width of the track, going into a shallow turn to the right. O'Bryan was concentrating on Johnny, hoping for the inside left lane. Jack moved up on his tail, established a draft for a mere second, but it was enough.

A bump.

Suddenly O'Bryan was careening out of the path, and Jack was zooming past him on the left.

The rest of the pack faded in the rearview mirror. There were only two cars in the race now.

Jack Dolman and Johnny Rendisi. Father and son.

REAR VISIBILITY was limited, but Johnny didn't need a panoramic view to realize there were only two of them vying for first place. Two laps to go, and all he could see was the helmet hiding his old man's eyes. He could easily imagine the vicious gleam in them.

Turn Six, shallow. Nonthreatening.

Seven. A hundred-degree left turnaround.

They shot onto the straightaway.

Jack was on his tailpipe. Johnny shifted right, then left.

More loose turns, short straight lines. They approached infamous Turn Eleven.

"This is where we separate the men from the boys, Jack," Johnny muttered in his mind.

He came from the outside of the curve to the inside as they whipped around the switchback. It was all familiar territory to Johnny, yet markedly different. Stock cars were heavier than open-wheel vehicles, and their tires were different. NASCAR used slicks—ungrooved wide tires that gave full contact with the road surface. Formula 1 used tires with four grooves that loosened their traction and facilitated skidding through sharp turns. The result demanded very different driving skills.

Johnny checked his mirror and couldn't believe the other car was still there, sucking his exhaust.

They maneuvered a long zigzag. Jack hung on close behind him.

"Get off my butt, old man," Johnny muttered.

The pack seemed a hundred miles behind them.

He spiraled through the treacherous Turn Eleven, the jackknife, but even with his right foot mashed to the floorboard he couldn't shake the car in his mirror.

The white flag. One lap to go.

Jack was like flypaper stuck to the sole of his foot. Johnny couldn't shake him.

They hit the longest straightway. Johnny hogged the inside.

"I won't give an inch, Jack," he shouted in his brain.

Jack rode his bumper. Johnny could feel the surge of the draft, and the lightness in his tail. Dammit.

He had no alternative but to slip to the right to break the draft, but Jack followed him.

"You're supposed to hold the inside, you fool." Johnny moved farther right, convinced his nemesis wouldn't follow.

But Jack did.

"What the hell are you doing, old man?" Johnny had to escape the draft's slipstream before Jack bumped him. He scooted to the left. Jack followed.

Then Johnny made his mistake. He rebounded to the right to break the draft.

This time Jack slingshotted on the newly opened left and shot forward as they entered the last left turn. All of a sudden Johnny was behind his father instead of in front of him, the pursuer instead of the pursued.

He pounded the steering wheel as he watched the checkered flag fluttering ahead of him and Jack Dolman zooming triumphantly under it.

CHAPTER FOURTEEN

"THIS IS YOUR FIRST WIN at this track," reporter Larry Waring noted, as he stood close beside Jack so they could both fit into the camera lens. They'd already gone through the Victory Lane formalities and were finally winding down. Winning was always exhilarating, but as the adrenaline waned, exhaustion replaced it. "How does it feel?"

"Absolutely great. This track isn't just a fun course but a real challenge."

"There were more cars eliminated in this one race than in the last six combined. How do you explain that?"

Jack grinned. "Right turns. We're all programmed to turn left."

The reporter chuckled with him. "Except for one driver," he said. "The one you beat, Johnny Rendisi, is used to making right turns from his Formula 1 days." He tilted the microphone toward Jack for a comment.

"Every race is different. Johnny ran a terrific race today, took the pole and stayed in front throughout most of the race, absolutely dominated the field."

"But you outsmarted him in the last few seconds."

Jack smiled humbly. "The ending could certainly

have been different." He knew his son was either watching the interview in real time or would soon see it in replay, and he didn't want to rub it in. "I was also lucky. We can't forget the role luck plays in any race."

"You've definitely had your share of good fortune in your career," the reporter agreed. "Next week is Daytona, where you've traditionally done very well. In fact you've had more wins on that track than on any other. Do you think your luck is going to hold?"

Jack's grin broadened. "I certainly hope so. To make sure, though, I plan on racing my hardest, give Lady Luck a reason to smile on me."

The reporter turned to the camera and went into his monologue, giving Jack a chance to slip away. He saw Margaret in the second row of the group of spectators and wanted desperately to motion her over to stand by his side, but not in front of the press. He and Margaret had enough going on in their lives without trying to tackle them in a media spotlight. They walked parallel to each other toward his motor home. Another reporter, this one from the print media, stopped him. He nodded to Margaret to keep going. They would meet in his coach. Two minutes later, after answering the reporter's questions, Jack resumed his trek.

Margaret was standing in the living room, the TV remote in her hand, concentrating on the screen. He came up beside her, wrapped his arm across the small of her back and kissed her gently on the temple. She smiled without looking at him, her attention riveted on the images on the TV. Her attitude was a little deflating. He'd just won a difficult race against his own son, and she was practically ignoring him. Then he glanced at the giant screen and understood why.

A well-known sports program host was talking with Amber. She was gushing about what a great driver Johnny was.

"You must be very disappointed that he didn't win today, especially since this is more like the type of track he's used to."

She made a face pooh-poohing the idea. "This is just a minor setback," she was saying. "He's going to win the NEXTEL Cup. You'll see. I mean it's not like his father beat him by a mile. It was only a couple of seconds."

The reporter's face went completely still. "His father?" he asked in bewilderment. "Are you telling us Jack Dolman is Johnny Rendisi's father?"

Amber became instantly flustered. It was clear she hadn't realized what she was saying.

"Dammit, Amber," Margaret muttered and hung her head.

Jack closed his eyes and took a deep breath.

"Well, only in the biological sense," Amber said defiantly. "It's not like Dolman brought him up or anything."

The reporter recovered quickly, though it was clear he'd been thrown off balance by this bombshell. "So who was Antonio Rendisi?"

"His stepfather, of course, but Johnny has always thought of him as his real dad. I mean he's the only daddy he ever knew."

"Shut up, Amber." Margaret muttered between her teeth. "Please, baby, just shut the hell up."

"Too late," Jack said fatalistically. "The harm's done. We can't unring the bell."

Margaret bit her lips. "I'm sorry, Jack—" she placed her hand on his arm "—I'm so sorry."

He hugged her against him, aware of the feel of her warm softness. "It's not your fault. It was bound to come out sooner or later. I didn't expect it to be this way, but…"

Tears flowed down Margaret's cheeks. "I wish I could send her to her room."

He cracked an ironic smile. "With or without her dinner?"

"It's not funny." She looked so miserable, as if all of this were her fault.

He turned fully toward her and gently bracketed her shoulders. "You know something? The only thing that matters to me right now is that I love you."

She gazed up at him, startled, her jaw slack, her eyes peering at him in wonder and surprise.

He gave her a playful grin. "Now you're supposed to say you love me, too. Unless you don't, of course."

She threw her arms around him and gripped him tightly. Resting her head against his chest she sobbed as the tears began to fall.

"Hey, now. No need for that."

"I love you, Jack."

He kissed her then, long and hard. There was rapping. The media, he supposed, but he knew he'd locked the door behind him when he came in, because he'd wanted to be alone with this woman. He ignored the knocking and the calling and led her to the shower.

"I need you to wash my back," he murmured in her ear.

She grinned up at him. "Is that all? I bet I can do better than that."

"It's a place to start."

She brushed him with her hand. "I don't think starting is going to be a problem."

Eventually the clamor outside ceased, or he just didn't hear it.

"WHAT IN THE NAME OF GOD were you thinking?" Johnny shouted at Amber.

He'd come back to his motor home after enduring a dozen or more interviews by media wonks, all questioning how he could possibly have lost the road-course race to a guy who had never come in better than seventh on that track in his life. He'd been polite, even blasé, if not jovial about it, a good sport, but keeping a smile on his face had been like chewing glass. Five minutes after the last members of the press corps had shoved off, Mac told him about Amber's slip of the tongue. Fortunately the reporters didn't know about it when they were interviewing him or he'd still be there trying to explain his relationship with the driver who had beat him.

"I didn't mean—" she began defensively.

"You didn't *mean!*" He threw up his hands. "You didn't *think*, Amber. You just ran off at the mouth without giving any thought to the words you were spouting or the impact they would have."

"Stop yelling at me," she shouted back from the refrigerator where she'd been getting out a pop. She slammed the door and stomped across the room, banged her unopened can of soda on the coffee table, sprawled across the length of the couch, crossed her arms and stared defiantly up at the ceiling.

He paced furiously back and forth in front of the wide plasma screen, stopped, studied her a few seconds, then growled, "Dammit, look at me, Amber. Sit up straight and look at me."

She glared at him. "Don't talk to me that way. I'm not a child."

His menacing glower made clear he held a different opinion.

Mumbling incoherently under her breath, she shifted around, put her feet on the floor, stiffened her back and again crossed her arms. "There. Satisfied?"

"You screwed up royally today, Amber." His voice was no longer raised, but it was brittle with rage.

"What's the big deal?" She shrugged her shoulders petulantly. "So people know Jack Dolman's your father? I mean, everybody's got a father. I don't know why you want to make such a big secret of it."

"That's not the point. You had no right to blab to the whole world. If either of us wanted people to know about our relationship, it was our right to tell them, not yours."

She sighed dramatically. "I don't know what difference it makes."

He closed his eyes and considered that. "No, you don't, and that's precisely the problem. I have a right to privacy just like you. I also have a right to chose who I associate with."

He wasn't sure if it was his words or the quiet, almost

threatening tone in which he delivered them, that finally got through, but this time, when she met his eyes, she seemed to cringe.

"So I'll make a deal with you, Amber. If you want to continue to hang out here, if you still want to be my girlfriend, you have to keep your mouth closed with the press. No interviews. No background discussions with reporters or other media types at all. None."

"But…what do I say when they ask me questions? I can't just ignore them?"

"Be polite, talk about the weather, but don't get into a discussion about me, about Jack Dolman, about our relationship. You don't talk about our records, our teams or anything else. Got that?"

"It's going to be awfully hard because that's all they'll want to talk about."

He was tempted to ask her whose fault that was. "Just don't respond. Change the subject."

She sighed again. "Okay, I'll try."

"Trying won't hack it, Amber. You either do as I say or we're finished."

She stuck out her chin. "Who do you think you are, telling me what I can do and what I can say to people?" In spite of the belligerent tone, he could hear her apprehension.

"I'm the guy who's paying the bills, remember? If you don't like the conditions of my largesse, there's the door. Don't let it hit your pretty backside on the way out."

Her eyes went wide in shock. He could see she was also scared. "Aw, Johnny…" she pleaded, reverting to the coy young girl.

"And one other thing, sweetheart. Knock off the substances."

Her eyes went wide and for a second she bit her lips before asking in a low voice, "What do you mean? I don't know what you're talking about. I'm not—"

"Don't play games with me, Amber. I'm not in the mood for lies. You stay clean or you're out of here. I told you, I'm not about to throw away my career and reputation on some junkie. You do or say anything to embarrass me again and you're history. Got that?"

She worked her mouth, wanting to argue with him, to defend herself, but apparently she couldn't figure out what to say. She bit her lower lip, chin trembling, her eyes moist with tears.

At the moment he didn't care. He was beginning to seriously wonder what he'd ever seen in this woman… girl, really. He should have realized the difference in their ages would matter. But in Italy she'd been so mature, so sophisticated. Since coming home to the States it was as if she'd reverted to a teenager again. A teenager with a gorgeous body, to be sure, and heaven help him, she knew how to use it. Sometimes she could be so sweet he just wanted to hold her in his arms, feel the softness of her skin and inhale her feminine scent. But she was going down the wrong path, abusing herself and everybody around her.

"There's no in-between, Amber. No middle ground. No halfway measures. You either clean up your act and stay clean, or we're through."

She bowed her head, and he saw a tear tumble into her folded hands. She ignored it, and he wished he could, too, but as angry as he was with her, he couldn't bear to see a woman cry.

Resisting the temptation to take her into his arms and soothe her, he sat on the edge of the chair opposite her. He knew what would happen if he touched her, and once they started there would be no stopping.

"Look, honey," he said after a pause, "if you need help, all you have to do is say so, and I'll give you whatever it takes. I mean that. I really care about you, *bellissima,* and your mom does, too. Stop and think about what all this is doing to her."

"She can take care of herself," Amber muttered.

The coldness of her response riled him anew. He stared at her for a long minute. "Your mother loves you and you don't even realize it."

He got up, shoved his hands in his pockets, stared down at the carpet and paced back and forth before speaking to her.

"If I thought you were clearheaded right now I'd kick your butt out of here, out of my life."

She raised her tearstained face. "Johnny…"

"Go to bed, Amber. Get some rest, sleep as long as you need to. Then, after you've had time to think about what I've said, we can talk." He turned toward the door.

"Where are you going?" Panic trembled in her question.

"I have a meeting with Steiner. He's leaving first thing in the morning. I need to discuss damage control with him."

"I…I'm sorry, Johnny." She was biting her lips, a lost, scared little girl.

He went over to her, pulled her into his arms, stroked her back. "I know, *cara*. Now get some sleep. I'll see you in the morning."

CHAPTER FIFTEEN

"WHAT'S THIS ABOUT Jack Dolman being your father?"
Steiner asked, after Johnny had closed the door. His
tone was none-too-friendly.

Johnny shrugged. "It's true."

Steiner sat behind the small desk in the corner of the
living room of his hotel suite. He didn't invite Johnny
to sit. "I think I deserve an explanation."

"He and my mother divorced when I was four years
old. Until he showed up at the cemetery for my mother's
burial, I hadn't seen him in twenty-five years."

"I don't like being used, Rendisi," he said quietly. "I
don't like being caught off guard by the media, and I
don't appreciate being taken for a fool."

"I haven't used you, Mr. Steiner."

On previous occasions they'd been on a first-name
basis, but Mac had warned Johnny that when Steiner
lowered his voice he was seething. At home it had
always been the other way around. There, when people
got angry, they threw temper tantrums, loud, bellowing
rants that everyone near and far could hear. His mother
used to throw things, too, though it was never at anyone.
It was just for emphasis, like a punctuation mark.

"Let's not play games, Rendisi. You intentionally withheld information."

"I didn't think it was important."

"Bull," Steiner snapped back almost before the last word was completely out. "Jack Dolman isn't a taxi driver or the guy who sells souvenirs out of the back of a truck. He's one of the biggest names in NASCAR. I don't know if you're intentionally lying to me, trying to hide your screwup or so damn stupid you don't know what's important and what's not."

Johnny's blood pressure rose. He wasn't used to being spoken to this way, and he didn't like it. Just because Steiner was the team owner didn't give him license to treat him like a servant.

"This may come as a surprise to you," Steiner continued, "but I really don't give a damn how you feel about your father. Love him, hate him. It's all the same to me. But you blindsided me. You held back information I had a right to know because it affects the public relations of this enterprise."

Steiner pushed back his chair, climbed to his feet and strode to the picture window overlooking the hills surrounding the Los Angeles valley. After a minute he executed an about-face and made full eye contact.

"When you first came to me six months ago and said you were interested in driving for Steiner Racing in the NEXTEL series because you wanted a new challenge, I had a feeling you weren't telling me everything. I didn't press you at the time. I respected your privacy with the expectation that at some point, if it was important, you'd be more forthcoming. I can see I made a mistake."

"Look—"

"Shut up. When I'm finished with my say, you can have yours."

Johnny was startled at the man's sharpness.

"It's clear you don't like your father," Steiner continued in his eerily low voice. "The reasons for your animus are your business, but it's also now apparent you're racing in the NEXTEL Series as part of some sort of personal vendetta against him. Again the specifics are your business and not in themselves of any concern to me—unless they impact the good name of Steiner Racing or NASCAR. Do they?"

Johnny's chest pounded. The Rendisi name in Italy, throughout Europe and in the world of Formula 1 meant something, demanded respect. He resented being talked down to like a hireling. Biding his time, he said only, "No."

"You're a good driver," Steiner acknowledged. "You still have a lot to learn, but you have talent and intelligence and a very promising career ahead with NASCAR, if you really want it." Steiner dropped into his seat and looked up. "I was hoping it would be with Steiner Racing, but I'm beginning to have second thoughts."

Johnny's anger instantly mutated to fear.

If Steiner dropped him now his career in NASCAR would be in serious trouble, maybe over. Steiner Racing was only a couple of years old, but it had a good reputation, having taken the NASCAR NEXTEL Cup in its first year of operation, but mostly because Steiner himself was highly regarded as a driver and as a man of integrity. Being dropped before the season was over would be a hard rap to overcome in future bids for a team and sponsors. It would also crush any hope Johnny had of defeating his father at his own game.

"Mr. Steiner, I'm sorry," he said, lowering his head and almost choking on the words. "You're right. I should have told you he's my father. I apologize."

The room remained quiet, but for the slight buzz of a quartz clock on a side table.

"Sit down." Steiner motioned for him to pull up the chair on the other side of the entertainment center.

"The question now is what we're going to do about this situation. The media are going to be all over it. When exactly were you planning on releasing the information?"

"I wasn't."

"You and your father have agreed to keep it secret?"

"We haven't discussed it."

"I said it was none of my business, and I repeat that, but I would like to know something of the background, if you're willing to tell me."

"Not much to tell, really. As I said, my parents were divorced when I was small, and I had no contact with my father until he appeared at my mother's interment."

"Was it a particularly acrimonious divorce? The press will uncover it, if it was."

"Not that I know of. My mother moved to Italy, divorced him, then later married Antonio Rendisi, who formally adopted me and gave me his name. Jack Dolman never raised any objections."

Steiner studied him, his eyes searching, and stroked his chin.

"Since the secret is out, how about a joint news conference?" he asked. "You and your dad together—"

Johnny was shaking his head before Steiner even finished his sentence. "No."

"What then?"

"We go on the way we have been. He hasn't said anything negative about me, nor have I about him."

"I'm not sure the press is going to let either of you off that easily. And what about your girlfriend?"

"She'll keep her mouth shut." He hadn't intended the words to come out so sharply.

"I guess that's the best we can hope for right now." Steiner rose to his feet.

Johnny did the same.

On their way to the door, Steiner extended his hand. "I'm not the enemy, Johnny," he said, "and I'd like to be your friend. Just be honest with me. If you have any other secrets I should know about—"

"I don't."

"LET'S TALK." Cal Farnsworth stood at the door of Mac Roberts's hotel suite.

Mac nodded, stepped aside and invited his visitor in. Neither would call the other a close friend. They didn't pal around together or share confidences over drinks on a regular basis, but they were professional colleagues who had no grounds to dislike each other and had plenty of reasons for mutual respect.

Cal stepped into the small living room.

"Want something to drink?"

Cal eyed the half-empty beer bottle sitting on the

edge of the counter that divided off the kitchenette. "One of those would do."

Mac went around to the three-quarter-sized refrigerator, removed a brew and handed it over. "Bet I know what you're here to talk about."

"Thanks." Cal twisted off the cap and swallowed a mouthful of the premium beverage. "Yeah. There aren't many secrets left these days."

"Did you know?" Mac waved him to the couch and took the chair opposite him. They sat.

"Jack and I go back a long way," Cal responded. He gave a concise version of what happened between his friend and Johnny's late mother. "It all happened long before I started working with Jack. I never met Lillah, and so I've gotten only one side of the story."

"But you believe him?" Mac asked.

"I've never known Jack to lie."

"The media are going to have a field day with this. You realize that."

"I know fire needs fuel and oxygen. It'll die out if we don't feed it."

Mac sipped his beer. "I'm not sure that's true in this case. Our people are going to want to make the most of this free publicity opportunity."

"I'm hoping you won't let them."

The other crew chief studied him. "What makes you think I have any say?"

"Look," Cal said, waving the lip of the beer bottle enough to emphasize his point, "I know you can't control the media, but you can influence Steiner and the PR people who work for him."

"You're asking a lot. What do we get in return?"

"To keep your reputation."

Mac raised his eyebrows. "Cal, I hope I'm not hearing you right, because that sounds an awful lot like a threat."

"No threat. That's not my style. My point is this, if we get caught up in a media feeding frenzy, we'll all get gnawed. Reporters aren't afraid to bite the hand that feeds them. In the end neither of us will come out unscathed."

"No argument there." Mac lifted his bottle to his lips but kept his eyes focused on Cal as he took a draw. "What do you have in mind?"

"Jack is probably going to retire at the end of this season. I don't imagine that'll come as a great surprise to anyone. Whatever brush you paint him with won't matter, leastways not for long, because he'll be gone. I'm asking you not to besmirch the reputation of a guy who has earned the respect and admiration of a lot of people. Take the high road. When he's gone you can expect to pick up some of his fans. Trash him and I can pretty much guarantee they're not going to transfer their allegiance to Steiner Racing."

Cal tipped his bottle, took a swing. "On the other hand," he continued, "your new guy is still building a fan base. They love his looks, his charm, the cultured European way he talks. But the mystique could evaporate quickly if the public gets to thinking of him as an interloper, a foreigner, an ungrateful son, someone who spends his time with druggies."

"Are you accusing Rendisi of taking drugs?" Mac's voice hardened. "Because if you are, you better have proof."

Cal shook his head. "I know you and Steiner well enough to realize neither of you would tolerate substance abuse, but we both know Rendisi's girlfriend may not be as clean as he is, and that doesn't reflect well on Steiner Racing—or NASCAR, for that matter."

Mac expanded his chest and climbed to his feet. For a moment Cal thought he was about to be thrown out. Instead, Mac went behind the counter, dropped his empty bottle in the trash and retrieved another from the refrigerator.

"You ready?" he called out.

Cal held up his half-full bottle. "I'm fine."

Mac wrenched the top off his fresh brew and came back to his chair. This time rather than sit, he stood behind it.

"This still sounds like a threat to me," he said.

"I'm not threatening you or anyone else, Mac. I've got too damn much pride to lower myself to that tactic. All I'm trying to tell you is what our PR people will do if your PR people try to exploit this. And for what? Gossip doesn't win races, and that's the business we're both in, winning races. Regardless of who takes home the Championship in November, whether it's Dolman or Rendisi or someone else, let's still have our dignity."

Mac paced. After several minutes he stopped and faced his visitor. "What do you propose?"

"That we agree not to give this story legs. You talk to your people and I talk to mine, and whenever reporters bring up the subject we simply don't respond. Change the subject. Talk about accumulated points, track conditions, the problems of running loose or tight, the last lousy pit stop we had, anything. It may not work, but my guess is if we're consistent, the issue will die a natural death. When the vultures realize they're not going to get any more out of us, they'll find something or someone else to peck at."

Mac swung around and resumed his seat. After a long pull on his beer, he sat there and considered the other man for yet another minute. "It's worth a try."

Cal nodded. "It may not keep other people from running off at the mouth—"

"If you're worried about Amber, don't. My gut feeling is that Rendisi will issue a gag order, if he even keeps her around."

Cal rose. "Thanks for the beer." He put his nearly half-full bottle on the end of the counter. "I'm sorry we had to have this conversation," he said, extending his hand.

Mac took it. "Yeah, me, too."

CHAPTER SIXTEEN

"JACK, WHAT CAN YOU tell us about your relationship with Johnny Rendisi?" the reporter asked.

He and his cameraman had popped out of a van parked not too far away the moment Jack opened his car door at the Charlotte track. It was late Tuesday morning. Jack had just flown into Daytona from Greensboro.

"Is it true Johnny Rendisi is your son?" Larry Waring asked as he ran alongside Jack, holding out a microphone.

"He's a fantastic driver, isn't he?" Jack replied, not breaking stride as he moved swiftly toward the track office. "It's tough making the transition from Formula 1 to stock, but he's done it. His record for a rookie in NASCAR is really impressive. Four wins so far and plenty of points going into the Chase."

"Were you and Johnny's mother married to each other when he was born?"

That question almost stopped him. Jack had never initiated physical violence against another person, but he briefly considered changing his policy. He was also tempted to blurt out that his son was definitely legitimate, but of course that would be giving Larry Waring exactly what he wanted.

"Open-wheel is so different from stock car racing," he said, as he hurried along. His legs were longer than the reporter's who was practically running to keep up. Jack didn't imagine the cameraman was getting a very stable picture as he did the same.

"A little like going from fixed-wing to rotary-wing aircraft, I guess," Jack speculated. "Of course I'm not a pilot, so I don't really know, but from people I've talked to, it seems to be an apt comparison."

"Did you leave his mother or did she leave you? Did you fight for custody of your son?"

They'd reached the area where the track office was located. Fortunately there was a security guard on duty to limit access.

"Got to go, guys," Jack said casually. "Probably see you in Daytona. That's always been a special track for me, and I'm looking forward to the challenge."

He waved to Larry Waring as he nodded to the guard and rushed on. He could feel the reporter's disappointment. Tough. He wouldn't get any newsworthy quotes out of that interview. Eventually he'd probably have to give definitive answers to specific questions, but for now he might as well enjoy evasion.

"HAVE YOU ALWAYS KNOWN who your biological father was?" Larry Waring asked Johnny as he stepped out of his limousine. Johnny hadn't anticipated being followed to the airport, but he probably should have. The media were persistent when they thought they had a hot story.

"He's an incredible driver, isn't he?" He extended his hand back into the passenger compartment and helped

Amber emerge. She had dressed modestly this morning, was quiet and very much like the young lady he'd been smitten with in Italy.

He tucked her arm protectively under his and moved toward the entrance to the lounge for private plane owners and passengers.

"Dolman has one of the best records in NASCAR."

"Is that why you switched from open-wheel to stock car racing?" Larry asked. "So you could compete against your father?"

"Grand Prix is a whole 'nother world. Even the terminology is different, sometimes for the exact same things. The rules of the road and the tracks sure are different."

"Like this track in Sonoma," the reporter persisted. "You were favored to win the race because of your Formula 1 experience and ended up coming in second to your father, who had never won a race here before. How do you explain that?"

"He's a damn good driver." He patted Amber's hand and was surprised to realize it was cold. "He's won just about everywhere else. It's about time he won there, don't you think?"

"So the rivalry isn't personal?"

Johnny flashed his most fan-endearing smile. "I ran my best race, and obviously so did he. Who knows, next time the order might be different." He raised his shoulders in an amused shrug. "Or maybe not. I completely agree with what he said in an interview not long ago. Never count out luck."

"So you think he won because he was lucky?"

Johnny laughed. "I think he was lucky to win, and if

I had won I would have been lucky, too." There, try to unwind that one, Johnny thought, wishing the passenger lounge entrance were closer.

"Do you and he get together to work out strategies, tactics?"

Johnny gave him a pathetic look. "I think that'd be called conspiracy. We're on different teams, remember?"

They'd reached the sliding-glass doors, which now automatically opened.

"Hey, I really have to run." He smiled again, friendly, appreciative for the opportunity to chat with the reporter. "There's another race coming up, and I have a lot of work to do. See you in Daytona."

BY THE TIME Jack's private jet landed in Greensboro and Margaret got home late Monday afternoon she was ready to tear into her daughter for spilling the beans on Jack and Johnny's relationship. Jack insisted they had damage control in hand, but it wouldn't have been necessary if Amber had kept her mouth shut. On the other hand, why was their relationship being kept secret at all?

But that wasn't the point. It was up to them to reveal it, not her.

She pulled up the driveway, past the house to the one-car detached garage in back, only to find Amber's red Mustang—a gift from Johnny—blocking the entrance. Margaret had installed a single carport beside the garage three years ago for a second car, but Amber was hogging the pad in front of both of them.

Tired and upset, Margaret strode to the back door and stopped.

Brahms' Double Concerto.

So Amber had found the CDs. Margaret had been a little afraid she would either ignore them or throw them away.

Margaret stood on the back stoop for several minutes, letting the sweet harmony wend its way into her and work its calming magic.

Should she say anything about the music? Should she ignore it? Wait for Amber to say something? She wanted to encourage her daughter to pursue her musical interests, but how? The wrong word at the wrong time and she could just as easily discourage her.

Quietly she opened the back door, which wasn't locked, though it should be, and stepped inside. The volume was up pretty loud, and under other circumstances, she would have insisted Amber turn it down. But not today. Then she realized there was something different about the sound.

She moved into the living room and was stunned.

Amber was standing in the middle of the room, her violin tucked under her chin, playing along with the recording. Not perfectly, Margaret realized now. Occasional notes were off-key, the timing not exactly in sync, but the overall effect was good. Very good.

She leaned against the door frame and let the beautiful, haunting strains of the violin and cello steal their way into her frazzled nerves and soothe them. Her eyes were closed, a smile on her lips when she realized Amber was no longer playing. Margaret opened her eyes.

"Mom?" Amber said, more embarrassed, it seemed, at having been caught than annoyed.

"That was beautiful, honey," Margaret said, still smiling.

"I didn't hear you come in."

"I just got here. I'm so glad to hear you playing again."

"I'm really lousy." But she was clearly pleased at the compliment.

"I haven't heard you play in so long. You were wonderful." She stepped over and gave her daughter a kiss on the cheek. "I'm glad I brought down your fiddle. I was cleaning out the attic—"

Amber placed the instrument back in its case but left it open. She walked over to the CD player and lowered the volume.

"You ought to audition for the civic symphony. They're always looking for musicians—"

"Who can play. I haven't touched that thing in over three years."

Margaret felt as though she was walking on eggshells. "But you've still got it. I've always liked the way you play Brahms."

"Aren't you going to give me a hard time, too?"

No question about what. "Do I need to?"

"Johnny's mad at me."

"I imagine he is."

"He treats me like a child."

Margaret refused to take the bait. "Have you eaten? I could do with something. I just don't know what. Any ideas?"

"I'm in the mood for something spicy. We could call out for Thai."

"Great idea."

After they made their selections from the menu posted on the refrigerator door with magnets, Margaret called and ordered, then went out to the car and brought in her suitcase. She was tempted to ask Amber to move her Mustang so at least one of them could use the garage, but decided it wasn't that important. While she was unpacking, however, she heard an engine start, peeked out her upstairs bedroom window and saw Amber moving her Mustang, then pulling the Escort into the garage and closing the door.

"Thanks, honey," she said when she came downstairs.

Amber made a dismissive sound, just as the front door bell rang. Their food had arrived.

"I really screwed up," Amber said halfway through their supper.

"You made a mistake. I watched it on TV. The words were out before you realized what you were saying. I thought you recovered fairly well."

"Johnny wants me to zip my lip."

Margaret nodded. "Probably not a bad idea for a while." She smiled across the table. "He'll get over it."

"You think so?"

"You going to Daytona?"

It took a moment for Amber to appreciate the question. "He wants me to meet him at the airport Wednesday afternoon instead of Thursday morning, so he'll have extra time at the track to walk it."

Margaret smiled. "I think you ought to take your violin along."

"I could practice while he's off at meetings and things."

"Sounds like a plan."

"Miss Truesdale. Oh, Miss Truesdale."

Amber and Johnny had arrived at Daytona Wednesday evening, as planned, and were relieved when reporters didn't mob them at the airport. It dawned on her now that that might precisely have been the reason he'd wanted to come down early. He'd been nice to her after her screwup Sunday evening, but things between them weren't the same as before. He was nice like a friend now, not like a boyfriend.

Okay, so he was still mad at her. That was understandable, she supposed.

She wished he'd fight with her. At least then she'd know he cared. She'd almost picked a fight with him a couple of times, but then she caught herself. If he didn't care about her anymore, if he was being nice because he thought he should, getting him angry wouldn't do any good, probably just get her kicked out of his life altogether, and she didn't want that. She loved him.

"Amber, wait up."

She tried not to notice and hurried toward the entrance to the motor home lot. Once she made it there, she'd be safe.

"I'm glad I caught you."

The voice, nearly breathless, was right behind her, too close to ignore. She ordered herself to calm down, play it cool. After a deep sigh she stopped and spun around to find Larry Waring only a few yards behind her.

"Oh, hi, Larry. How are you?" She plastered a welcoming smile on her face.

Panting, the reporter stopped. "Whew." He took a

deep breath. "Going down to Rendisi's coach? I'll walk with you. I'd like to talk to him, too, if he's there."

Amber almost asked "About what?" but realized in time she'd be leaving herself wide-open if she did. "What are you doing here today? This is only Thursday. The race isn't till Sunday."

"I always come early. For background interviews."

"I'm surprised anybody has time with so many preparations under way."

"Sometimes they don't. You have to take your chances. What I wanted to ask you is how long you've known he and Dolman are father and son."

Amber didn't say anything. After all he hadn't actually asked a question, merely said what the question would be when he did ask it. Didn't make any difference. She wasn't going to tell him.

He frowned at her silence as they walked along. She didn't want to bring him into the motor home, like a guest. Johnny wouldn't be pleased. But the security guard wouldn't let him inside without her say-so.

"Well," Larry said, "at least tell me how they get along?"

She still didn't reply, and she could sense the guy's frustration. Sort of made her feel good. Powerful. Avoiding answering questions was kind of fun, she realized, like a game.

"Why all the secrecy? You'd think they'd be proud of each other. Or," he asked, as though the idea had just struck him, "has this all been a publicity stunt to get attention?"

Amber regarded him as if he were crazy, but she still didn't say anything.

"When were they going to spring this on their fans? At the last minute, maybe just before the final race, or maybe after it?"

They had reached the security entrance.

"Can I come with you?" Larry asked, eyeing the guard.

"No, sorry, I just remembered I need to do something for Johnny."

"What are you talking about?"

"Corn bread. I need to make corn bread. Johnny never had it in Italy, and he's decided he really likes it, so I'm going to make him some."

"Corn bread? You're pulling my leg, right?"

"They don't make corn bread in Europe. Did you know that? In fact a lot of people over there, especially the older generation, don't even eat corn. Can you imagine? Life without corn on the cob slathered with butter, salt and pepper. Sometimes I put too much pepper on it and have to wipe it off. Have you ever done that?"

"Amber? Come on. Give me a break," he pleaded, realizing at last he wasn't going to get answers from her to any of his questions.

"I'm going to make Johnny corn bread with crackling in it. That's the best kind. My favorite." She showed the guard her credentials and walked through the entrance. Alone. "See you later, Larry."

CHAPTER SEVENTEEN

JACK AND HIS SON played leapfrog with each other for the next eight races. Jack won at Daytona, came in second at Chicago and third at Pocono. Johnny came in first at Watkins Glen, the other road course, redeeming himself for Sonoma, as well as at Michigan the following weekend. Pointwise they continued to be neck and neck, which added another irony. Hauler positions in the infield were based on points. That meant father and son continued to park side by side, which definitely interfered with Johnny's determination to remain aloof from his father. With their work areas cheek by jowl it was impossible for the two not to run into each other, at least in passing. They could hardly ignore one another without appearing, as Margaret had pointed out, uncivilized.

At first their exchanges were no more than polite greeting. "Good morning." "Nice day." But slowly Jack began upping the ante. He started making comments about the condition of the track they were at and gradually worked in offhand advice, always obliquely given. He didn't tell Johnny to watch the grooves on the inside of Turn Two or the banking out of Turn Four. Rather it was "I was hoping they'd resurfaced the inside of Turn Two. The grooves there have gotten really treacherous." Or "Seems like there are more spinouts on the front stretch at this track than anywhere else. Probably because of the banking out of Turn Four. The fans love it, of course."

And it was always good advice. It seemed that in spite of himself, Johnny began looking forward to Jack's comments, though he was always leery of them.

A press conference was called the day after the Richmond race. Jack had come in third. Johnny had been a distant seventh, good enough, though, for both of them to make the cut for the Chase for the NASCAR NEXTEL Cup Championship. Lined up against the wall behind the podium in the press room were Jack's team owner, Douglas Habersham, his team chief, Caleb Farnsworth, his press agent, Andrea Tompkins, as well as several members of the garage team.

Missing was his son, Johnny Rendisi.

Jack stood at the cluster of microphones in his racing uniform, all smiles and confidence, and waited patiently for the room to quiet down.

"Thank you all for coming," he said when it finally did. "My announcement will be brief, then I'll be glad to answer your questions."

Another pause and the chatter ceased altogether. "As most of you know, I've been driving in NASCAR for a long time." He gazed out over his audience of attentive faces and grinned. "Longer than some of you have been alive."

Snickers throughout the room.

"I love NASCAR. It's been my life for over thirty years. It's also been good to me, earned me a lot of money and allowed me to live well. I like to think I've been good for NASCAR, too. I've chalked up a few trophies, a few championships. I won't remind you how many. That would be bragging, and as you all know, I'm a very modest guy."

"I must have been out sick that day," someone yelled out.

Everyone laughed. Jack grinned again.

"The point of all this nostalgia is that it's time for me to move on. From behind the wheel. I'm announcing today that at the end of this season I'll be climbing out of the driver's side window for the last time, at least as an active competitor."

Murmurs filled the room and camera flashes strobed. Jack could feel video cams zooming in. Several voices started calling out questions.

He held up his hands. "I have just a couple more things to say, then we can get to your questions."

The murmurs subsided.

He resumed. "There are so many people I need to thank for the wonderful experience I've had with NASCAR. I don't know where to start and probably wouldn't know where to stop. So at the risk of offending people I don't mention, let me just name a few. First, my crew chief and my best friend, Caleb Farnsworth. We've been together on one team or another for about twenty years now. I can't imagine what it'll be like not having him giving me orders."

More chuckles.

Jack went through a litany of people he wanted to thank, from the Windsand team owner, Doug Habersham, to members of his pit team.

"Finally, let me make it clear that even though I'm retiring from driving I'm not leaving NASCAR. NASCAR racing is in my blood. It'll always be a part of me, so I plan on contributing to it for as long as I can." More flashes went off. He smiled as the clamor began. "Now I'll take your questions."

"Do you have any health problems that have influenced your decision?"

"Nope. I get regular physical checkups, and the doc tells me I've got the body of a twenty-year-old. Okay—" he smirked "—maybe he said thirty. All I know is I feel great."

"Does the fact that your son, Johnny Rendisi, is now competing against you have anything to do with your decision?"

Jack shook his head. "I'm fifty years old, the oldest driver on the track, in a sport where most of my competitors are in their twenties and thirties—"

"Have you discussed this decision with your son?" Larry Waring asked. "How does he feel about it?"

Someone else called out, "Why isn't he here?"

In trying to anticipate questions, Jack had considered these and would have liked to say they'd talked it over, that Johnny fully supported him, but it wasn't true, and if he ever hoped to mend fences with his son, fabricating stories about their relationship wouldn't help matters.

Cal had called Mac Roberts the night before to tell him about the announcement this afternoon, and he'd suggested it would be nice if Johnny attended the news conference. He wouldn't be asked to say anything unless he wanted to. Mac had agreed to pass the information on. Jack was confident he had; he also wasn't surprised his son hadn't shown up.

"Johnny knows about my plans," was all he said. He saw an older reporter, one who in the past had been fair and evenhanded, put up a finger. Jack pointed to him.

"You said you don't intend to leave NASCAR. Can you tell us more about your future plans?"

Doug Habersham, the team owner, stepped up to the mic.

"As you know Jack has been driving for Windsand Motorsports for the last eight years, and I've been proud to have him as part of our team. I'm also pleased to announce he's agreed to stay on with us as a consultant. Nothing teaches like experience, and Jack Dolman has over thirty years of incredible success in stock car racing to draw upon."

"So you're not going to be coaching or advising your son in his NASCAR career?" Larry Waring called out.

Another question to be avoided, but Jack knew it couldn't be.

"At the moment we're on separate teams. That could change in the future, of course."

"Jack," a friendly voice called out, "can you tell us about the relationship you share with your son? It seems like all our questions to either of you result in nothing but double-talk. Now, today, you're announcing what must be one of the most significant events in your life and he's not here. Rather than force us to indulge in all kinds of speculation, can you give us the straight scoop?"

The room became silent, and Jack realized there was no way to evade any longer.

He crunched up his mouth for a moment, and nodded his head. "Fair enough."

Bracing his hands on the podium, he said, "Johnny's mother and I divorced when he was four years old. She moved to Italy and later married internationally famous Formula 1 driver, Antonio Rendisi, who adopted Johnny and introduced him to the world of Grand Prix racing. The rest is well documented. Johnny became a star in his own right, and I couldn't be more proud of him."

"Did you keep in contact with him over the years?" someone else called out.

Jack hesitated, but there was no turning back. "We didn't see each other again until after his mother passed away."

"So you're strangers. Hostile strangers at that," another reporter opined.

"Strangers perhaps," Jack acknowledged. "But hostile? Definitely not. I have nothing but the greatest respect and admiration for my son's achievements."

"If you're friends, why isn't he here today?" an unpleasant voice demanded.

Cal Farnsworth stepped up to the mic. "You can blame that on me. I spoke with his crew chief, Mac Roberts, last evening. Unfortunately it was bad timing. Johnny already had other commitments, but he asked me to extend his best wishes."

Jack refrained from looking askance at his friend,

knowing the professional reporters there would pick up on it.

Andy Tompkins, Jack's press agent, stepped forward and insinuated herself between Jack and Cal.

"Thank you all for coming, ladies and gentlemen. As you can imagine we have a very tight schedule for the upcoming Chase for the NASCAR NEXTEL Cup. Next weekend we'll be in New Hampshire, followed by Dover, then Talladega, all building inexorably to the final match in Miami in November. It's been an exciting season so far. You can be sure the Chase is going to be even more exciting. We'll see you all there. Thank you again for coming."

Questions battered them, and like a politician campaigning for office, Doug Habersham stepped up to the mic and began talking about his great team and plans he had for Windsand Motorsports. Jack used the diversion to slip out the side door. Cal was right behind them.

Jack turned on him. "I don't think putting words in Johnny's mouth is going to make us any friends."

Cal took no offense at the tone. "I didn't, Jack. When you watch this news conference on TV later, listen carefully to what I said. I said I talked to Mac, that he said Johnny was unavailable, and he—Mac—sent his best regards."

"That wasn't the impression you gave."

Cal laughed. "It wasn't the impression I wanted to give. I was purposely ambiguous. They'll believe what they wanted to hear."

"Pretty slick. Suppose Johnny doesn't see it that way and says so publicly?"

"Then he'll come off as petty. Don't worry. He won't. He may not like you, but he likes himself more."

It was a harsh judgment that Jack resented. Coming from anyone else he would have challenged it, but Cal was his best friend, and harsh or otherwise, his evaluation was undoubtedly accurate.

Margaret joined them. She'd been standing quietly in the shadows at the back of the room and had ducked out when Jack had.

"You did fine," she said and kissed him softly on the cheek.

But he didn't feel fine. Even her touch couldn't heal the ache inside.

MARGARET WAITED until New Hampshire to challenge Johnny about not showing up at Jack's retirement announcement, though she preferred to think of it as a discussion rather than a confrontation. He had taken the pole on Friday, so she was sure he'd be in high spirits when she dropped by his motor home that evening. Jack, who'd nailed the third position, right behind his son in the opening lineup, was attending a meeting with his team.

Amber answered the knock on Johnny's door and grew stiff and wide-eyed when she saw it was not only her mother, but also that Margaret was carrying her violin case.

"What are you doing here?" she demanded. "And why did you bring that?"

"I figured you forgot it."

Johnny came to the door. "Hello, Margaret. I wondered when you'd be showing up." He gazed at the instrument case in her hand. "You planning to play Hearts and Flowers while you lecture me?"

The humor in his sarcasm was probably a good sign, she decided. "May I come in?"

He laughed. "Sure."

Amber's expression wasn't nearly as welcoming as she stepped aside.

"What's with the instrument?" he asked, eyeing it again. "Do you play?"

"Not a note. It's Amber's."

He looked over at his girlfriend. "You never told me you played the violin."

"I don't."

"She's a bit rusty right now," Margaret acknowledged, "since she hasn't practiced in a long time, but you should ask her to play for you. She's actually quite talented."

"Mom, dammit—"

"Don't speak to your mother that way," Johnny admonished her. Then he turned back to Margaret. "Is that all you came for? To deliver her violin?" They both knew it wasn't.

She hesitated. "And to ask you to encourage her to try out for our civic symphony back home."

"M-o-m," Amber pleaded and turned away.

"She's really very good when she works at it. Ask her to play Brahms for you."

"The lullaby?"

Margaret narrowed her eyes as she scrutinized him for an extended moment. "If going to bed is all you're interested in."

He flinched and turned toward the living room.

Margaret placed the instrument case on the marble counter. "I thought the news conference went very well. You were missed, of course, but I think Jack and his friends handled the situation well. It would have been much nicer and made *you* look better, if you'd shown up or at least released a statement of congratulations and support for your father's retirement."

Johnny's mood instantly shifted. "My father is dead."

She blinked slowly, shook her head and blinked again. "Your father is a living, breathing, feeling man, and you're an insensitive idiot. I'm beginning to see why you'd be attracted to a nineteen-year-old."

Amber's mouth fell open and Johnny glared. "I think you'd better leave," he said when he finally found his voice.

Margaret's heart was beating painfully, and her instinct was to run, but she didn't budge. She took a massively deep breath and let it out. "Not until I've said my piece. Jack Dolman didn't abuse your mother, Johnny, and he didn't abandon you."

"You don't know what you're talking about."

Margaret had never been an argumentative person, something she recognized now as a personal flaw. Perhaps if she'd been more forceful Gary wouldn't have made the bad choices he'd made and Amber would have more self-respect. Maybe, too, if she had been stronger and told Jack the uncomfortable truth years ago he wouldn't have let her go so easily.

But even weak people find a limit to their endurance, she decided, and she'd found hers.

"You continue to allow yourself to be blinded by an

unfaithful philanderer, even after your mother, who you claim to have loved, told you herself that Antonio was lying about your real father. Compare that with the man you've been racing against all these months, a man whose reputation is impeccable. Wake up, Johnny. Talk to the man. Listen to his side of the story."

Johnny's back stiffened, his jaw tightened and his lips compressed into a thin line. He strode determinedly to the door, yanked it open and held it. "Please leave."

Shaking her head, Margaret walked on wobbly legs toward him, paused to gaze up at his startlingly blue eyes—so like his father's—and stepped outside. The door latch snapped firmly behind her.

She was at the foot of the steps when she heard the door open again. She glanced back over her shoulder.

"And take this with you." Amber threw the violin case. It bounced and rolled once on the grass verge a few feet to the left and lay there upside down.

Close to tears, Margaret started to bend down to pick it up, then thought better of it. If Amber didn't retrieve it, Johnny would. Straightening her back, she marched with an aching heart toward Jack's motor home.

JOHNNY WON in New Hampshire and came in third at Dover. Jack won at Talladega, but came in seventh in Kansas. Johnny took second place in Kansas and at the track in Charlotte. The next race turned out to be a special challenge and his nemesis.

As Amber had learned from her research, only slightly longer than half a mile in length, Martinsville was the shortest track on the circuit, a few feet shorter than Bristol, not as steeply banked on the turns, and bumpy to boot. The track predated NASCAR itself and was the very antithesis of an open-wheel road course.

This was Johnny's second stab at it, and he did worse than he had the first time. With forty-three cars starting the race on such a short field, it wasn't long before it was impossible for Amber to tell who was leading the pack and who was following it. Opportunities for passing were extremely limited, making this ironically similar to a Formula 1 contest in which a good qualifying position was vital to a decent finish.

Johnny started off well enough, in eighth position, but consistently lost ground, finally finishing thirty-eighth, his worst performance all season, and from what she could tell he had no excuse for the poor showing. No tire, suspension or engine problems. No spinouts. No crack-ups.

He came away from the event angry and disheartened.

"Aw, honey, it's just one race," Amber said, putting her arms around his waist and pressing herself against him. "You're still miles ahead in points." She'd been keeping track of them lately, keeping quiet and to herself.

"I don't race for points," he snapped, removed her hands and stepped away. "I race to win."

"I know," she said softly, trying to sound sympathetic, "but the season isn't over yet. You still have plenty of time to win the Cup and beat your daddy."

"Dammit, Amber, how many times do I have to tell you not to call him that?"

She lowered her head and shook it slightly. She'd been trying so hard to do everything he asked of her, to be just like he wanted her to be, then without thinking she'd do or say something that would set him off.

"I'm sorry, sweetheart," she said. "I keep forgetting. I loved my daddy a whole lot, so it's hard for me to remember that it was different for you."

"Antonio was my father, as far as I'm concerned. He was my daddy, as you like to so quaintly refer to him."

She closed her eyes and opened them, took a breath and turned away. He was making fun of her again. Why did he have to do that?

"I'm sorry, *cara.* That was a cheap shot. I didn't mean it the way it came out."

She wanted to ask him how he did mean it, but decided to leave it alone.

He hadn't yelled at her in a long time now. In fact he'd been very loving, the way she'd dreamed he would be. She hadn't taken any medication lately, just as she'd promised, and she kept telling herself she wouldn't, but the thought of not taking it scared her, even more than his reaction when she did.

Maybe she could keep it from him.

She could probably go and stay with her mother for a few days, but that might be even worse. If her mom found the pills she'd take them away. She thought Amber had stopped taking them before they went to Italy, but she hadn't. She needed them sometimes because she was afraid of the pain.

If the pain came back they'd have to cut her and she'd lose Johnny. She couldn't do that.

Her mother didn't know Lillah's doctor had given her more of the pills when they were over there, but those had run out, too. That was all right, though. She still had the old ones.

"Come on, honey," she crooned. "Why don't you take a nice hot shower, and I'll give you a massage, the kind you like, to relax you?"

"Will you play your violin for me later?"

He'd retrieved it when she'd thrown it at her mother, then he'd tricked her into playing it for him by saying he didn't believe she knew how to. Actually, she'd let him think he'd tricked her.

She'd played a country-and-western song, then a piece by Tchaikovsky. Not very well, but he'd been impressed. Or said he was. She'd forgotten how much she enjoyed playing. She hadn't told him, but she'd been practicing when he was out.

"You really want me to?"

"I really want you to," he said smiling.

CHAPTER EIGHTEEN

THE MEDIA WERE GOING CRAZY over the competition between father and son. Feature stories were written about their diverse backgrounds. Larry Waring probed deeper and found dates, the marriage between Jack Dolman and Lillah Neace and the birth of their son, Johnny, seven months later. Lillah's uncontested European divorce from Jack four years after that, her marriage to Antonio Rendisi the following week. The bare facts weren't difficult for an experienced journalist to uncover. Subtracted from the circumstances shaping them, however, they gave a distorted view of the people involved and lent themselves convincingly to Johnny's misinterpretation of what happened.

Reading the summary of events in the sports section of her morning paper, Margaret wondered for a moment if Johnny himself might not have been the source of the information, but another moment's reflection convinced her otherwise. As liberal-minded as he was, he would hardly have welcomed public knowledge that he'd been conceived out of wedlock.

Of more concern to Margaret was the effect the publicity was having on Jack.

She was cleaning up the motor home's galley after dinner—she'd prepared trout amandine, one of his favorites—and he was flipping through TV channels, when she heard him mutter, "He doesn't know what the hell he's talking about."

She checked the screen and it was one of those sports-panel talk shows.

"There are a couple of schools of thought on this," Larry Waring was saying. "One is that Dolman and his son are actually pretty close and have been ever since the death of Antonio Rendisi a few years ago."

"You mean this feud, if that's what you want to call it, is little more than a publicity stunt?" asked Nel Tunis, the woman on the panel.

"A good one, if that's true—" Gilbert Santos laughed "—after all, we're sitting here talking about them."

"The other opinion," Waring went on, "is that the animosity is genuine. Jack Dolman never asked for custody of his son when he divorced Johnny's mother, and my sources tell me Johnny has never forgiven him for it."

The latter interpretation was almost correct. It was certainly closer to the truth than the publicity conspiracy theory, and Margaret wondered if there really was a source for Waring's speculation, and if that source might be Amber. She didn't want to believe it, but she couldn't totally dismiss the possibility.

"Larry Waring's been begging you for an interview since the story broke," she reminded Jack. "Why not give him one and spell out what really happened?"

He grunted, disdainful of the suggestion. "Do you seriously think that'll make me look better? I'll come across as so inept as a husband that my wife ran away with a foreigner, and so uncaring as a father that I never even bothered to put up a fight when she took my son from me."

"Not if you explain it to him the way you explained it to me," she argued.

"It'll sound like excuses."

"At least talk to Johnny about it then, set *him* straight. If he chooses not to believe you the blame is his, not yours."

"Drop it, Megs. I told you my reasons. It's a no-win situation."

"It is if you won't fight," she retorted.

He stared at her, and the hurt in his eyes told her she'd said the wrong thing. "Not fight?"

No point in backing off now, she thought. "If you won't talk to him—and I understand why you don't want to—then let me. He'll listen to me, Jack."

Despite their little face-off in New Hampshire, Johnny had been pleasant and polite when they'd met in public at Dover and Talladega. She admired that about him, his ability to disagree, even strongly, and still remain civil and friendly. Amber had been a credit to both her mother and Johnny over the last few weeks, dressing more appropriately and acting like the lady Margaret knew she was. Fearful of provoking another scene and wanting to give her daughter space, Margaret had nevertheless kept her distance.

"He'll listen to me," Margaret repeated. "I have nothing to gain."

"That's right, so stay out of it."

"Jack, I think you're making a mistake. Johnny has a right to hear your side of the story—"

"And I'm asking you again. Let it be." He glowered at her, as angry as he was hurt by her opposition.

She closed her eyes for a moment before saying fatalistically, "Okay, okay. But I still think you're making a mistake."

FATHER AND SON CONTINUED their game of catch-me-if-you-can in the last three races leading up to the final round in Miami.

Jack blew an engine in Atlanta, eliminating himself from the race midway through. Johnny came in second, putting him ahead by thirty-eight points, but Jack won in Texas, hurling Johnny back as front-runner by a squeaky six.

Neither of them won in Phoenix, but Jack and Johnny managed to finish fifth and sixth respectively. Pointwise they were separated by only ten, Jack still on top, but it was a fragile advantage. For all practical purposes they were in a dead heat.

Jack arrived at the Miami track on Thursday, keyed up and anxious. This would be his last race. Regardless of the outcome, in four days he would be retired, no longer a competitor in the sport that had dominated, even consumed most of his life.

One race to go.

Against his son.

While the hauler was being positioned, his green-and-yellow Number 424 car unloaded for the last time, the garage area set up with toolboxes and a myriad of equipment, Jack went to the wall, slung his legs over it and started walking the mile-and-a-half oval track. There were no cars on it yet, though the roar of engines being revved, tested and tuned echoed all around him.

He paced the rough textured asphalt, gazed over at the stands that would be crowded with over 60,000 cheering fans in a few days and tried to feel something: sadness, nostalgia, even relief. He was both disappointed and astounded when he realized he felt nothing. He should be torn by emotion right now, depressed at saying goodbye to a world to which he'd given so much time and energy. But he felt nothing, not even the hollowness of loss.

With a mental shrug he retreated into routine. He checked the condition of the track, noted the three-degree angle of the pavement in the straightway, looked ahead to the steeper banking of the curve ahead. There was no particular need for him to walk this course. He'd been here before. Many times. It was a good track but unremarkable in design, a regular oval a mile and a half long with shallow six-degree turns.

While he was on the outside straightaway he watched as haulers drove onto the infield. He didn't have to read the names on the sides of the 18-wheelers to recognize who they belonged to. Rafael O'Bryan's green-and-silver van. Jem Nordstrom's brown-and-gold. Others that were as familiar as old friends. He saw the black-and-silver of Steiner Racing pull up. Johnny's team had arrived, and if he wasn't with them, he soon would be.

Jack had been younger than Johnny was now when he'd first started racing in NASCAR, pitting himself against legendary drivers. As a rookie Jack hadn't been as well-known as the former Formula 1 champion was, though, and certainly not as wealthy.

Did his son feel the same sense of awe and excitement as he'd felt all those years ago? He couldn't imagine not experiencing the rush of adrenaline, the niggling fear that he might not measure up, the high of anticipation for the race ahead.

Jack had dreamed of someday sharing those emotions with his son. Sunday they would, but separately.

His last race. The last time he'd compete against others, against himself. The last chance to cross the finish line first, to tote the checkered flag and soak in the adulation of the crowd.

His last chance.

Jack had been mulling an idea in his mind for some time, but he still hadn't reached a conscious decision, though in his gut—no, in his heart—he knew what he would do. A far different farewell to his long career than he could ever have imagined.

JOHNNY DROVE his practice laps Friday. His engine was fine-tuned, his pit crew well practiced in their drills.

On Saturday he and his entire team had their usual prerace strategy meeting at noon. Johnny ate a light lunch of salad, then waited his turn to run his qualifying lap.

He took the pole. A good omen.

At least it would be in Grand Prix racing. But Grand Prix had become a distant memory. This was NASCAR. The rules weren't the same. The game was played differently. That much he'd learned over the long season.

He'd come to stock car racing expecting to do well. After all, he was an internationally-renowned racing star. It had taken him a while to realize how complacent and arrogant that attitude had been. He'd had to learn humility, something Antonio Rendisi had never taught him.

But Jack Dolman had.

Saturday evening Mac held their last team meeting. He reviewed the lineup. Rafael O'Bryan was number two. Jack Dolman number three, which placed him directly behind Johnny. Jem Nordstrom was on Jack's right, in the fourth spot. There were three other guys in the backfield Steiner warned him about and alerted his spotter to watch. They'd worked out their strategy for pit stops, discussed a few more details, then split.

"Big day tomorrow," Steiner commented as they exited the hauler. "The best advice I can give you right now is to get some sleep—" he chuckled "—if you can."

Sure. Right. With his nerves tingling, there wouldn't be much sleep tonight.

And he didn't have Amber with him. He'd found her high on something yesterday and thrown her out. It broke his heart but he had no choice. The last thing he needed was to have someone see him with her in that state. He had given her enough chances.

He arrived at the motor home and let himself in, plunked his keys on the counter and went to the refrigerator. He wasn't a drinker, but a cold beer right now might help him unwind.

There was a rap on the door.

Dammit. Probably Amber begging for another chance. He wished he knew what to do with her. She was driving him crazy. No woman had ever possessed him the way she did, or frustrated him so thoroughly. She was an impossible maze of contradictions, a vixen and an angel, a tiger and a kitten.

Another knock. Might as well get it over with.

He strode over and opened the door. But it wasn't Amber.

"WHAT ARE YOU DOING HERE?"

Jack stood on the platform outside the door. "May I come in?"

"Why?"

"Oh, loosen up. I don't bite. I haven't got a knife. I don't carry a gun. For a few minutes can we at least be civil to each other?"

Johnny stared at his father, muttered something in Italian, probably a profanity, pulled the door wide and stepped aside.

Jack entered the motor home.

"Now what do you want?"

He studied his son for a minute. So much anger.

No invitation to move farther inside or to sit down.

"Tomorrow is my last race, as you know. I plan on ending my career with a win."

Johnny refused to show any emotion.

"I've watched you, son. You've learned a lot. You're good. But if you're going to whip my ass tomorrow, you're going to have to do a whole lot better."

"And I suppose you're going to tell me how."

"As a matter of fact, I am. The question is whether you'll follow my advice."

"Why should I?"

"Because what I'm going to tell you is the secret to success." Jack paused a moment while he held the younger man's gaze. "And because I've never lied to you."

Johnny stared back at him incredulously. The last statement might be true, but only because they'd spoken so little to each other.

"Why don't you say whatever it is you've come to say and get the hell out of here?"

Jack moved over to the living room side of the counter, pulled out one of the stools and set a hip on it. "Like I said, you're good, but you have one major flaw. The bump-draft. You've drafted only three times this entire season."

His son's dark brows narrowed, the lines between them deepening.

"I've studied all the races, noted all the things you do, and don't do. You've drafted three times for very short periods, never more than thirty seconds, and you've never bumped. You've let yourself be drafted four times, and to your credit, after Nordstrom did a number on you at Vegas, you've avoided being bumped."

Johnny moved up to the corner of the counter, leaned against the green marble slab and crossed his arms. "What's your point?"

"You're afraid of the draft."

Johnny sucked in a sharp breath. "You don't know what you're talking about, old man."

Jack laughed. "Ah, but it's true. I understand why. You can't do it in open-wheel racing, so you've had no experience with it. You must know by now, though, that it works."

Johnny glared at him. Interesting, Jack thought, that he hasn't denied it. "And your point is?"

"Barring any unforeseen events, like getting caught in a pileup or blowing an engine, the race tomorrow is going to come down to a contest between you and me, son."

That was the second time he'd called him *son,* and he could see it didn't sit well, but after the "old man" crack Johnny could hardly complain.

"I understand there'll be a few other cars out there," Johnny commented wryly.

Jack chuckled. Humor, even cynical humor, was a positive step forward. At least, he hoped it was.

"They don't have the same stakes in the outcome you and I do. This will be my last hoorah, Johnny." It was the first time he'd addressed him by name, and amazingly it felt even more intimate and personal than calling him son. Johnny seemed to realize it, too, judging from the almost embarrassed expression on his face.

"You can be sure it's going to be pedal to the metal for me," Jack admitted. "And for you, you want to kick my butt so bad, you'll do anything, make a pact with the devil…maybe even take my advice."

Johnny shook his head. "You're crazy."

Jack gave a one-shouldered shrug. "Could be, but hear me out before you make your final judgment."

His son rolled his eyes and settled onto the stool at the other end of the counter. "Go on."

"By the last lap tomorrow, it's going to be you and me in front."

"You're sure about that?"

"I'm sure. I'm going to be in the lead, and you're

going to be right on my tail. The question is whether you'll have the guts to take full advantage of the opportunity that'll give you."

"Exactly what are you suggesting?"

Jack had the feeling his son already knew. He just wanted it spelled out. "Do you understand how the bump-draft works?"

"Now you're insulting me."

"No. Merely asking a question, since you've never used it, and you've had several chances to. In Daytona. In Chicago, and again in Michigan. Golden opportunities you passed up."

"It's a dangerous maneuver," Johnny blurted out defensively.

"Yep, in a tight pack in the hands of an amateur, it definitely is. So you were probably wise in blowing off the chances when you had them."

"You son of—"

"My, my. Are all Formula 1 drivers so thin-skinned?"

The only response was a smoldering glare, followed by a rocking of his head as he realized he'd been snookered.

"Anyway," Jack went on, "tomorrow the last lap will be ours. If you really want to win, there's only one way to do it. You're going to have to get on my butt, establish a draft and bump me."

"And you're just going to sit there and let me, I suppose."

"Hell, no." Jack snorted. "I'm going to be wiggling my tail all over the place, trying to keep you from succeeding, but if you're as skillful as you think you are, you only have to draft me for a second to bump me and send me spinning, then you can go on and take the checkered flag."

CHAPTER NINETEEN

JOHNNY SAT ON THE EDGE of the bar stool, studying his father. Was the guy serious? Did he actually think Johnny would believe he was telling him how to beat him? Johnny considered the strategy the old man had described. The strange part was that it made sense. It might actually work.

Or would it?

Jack had been right about a couple of things. Johnny was a novice at the draft, using it very briefly only three times, never comfortably, and he'd passed up several prime opportunities to employ the bump-draft. Both Steiner and Mac had been critical of him afterward for not following through. As much as Johnny wanted to deny it, he had to admit, at least to himself, that he was afraid...well, *cautious* about employing the technique. At Steiner's insistence he'd even practiced it with test drivers, but one-on-one with a teammate on an empty or near-empty track was different from applying it in a tight race closely surrounded by competitors. Too many of the tapes Johnny had reviewed showed spectacular multiple car pileups that resulted when the driver of the trailing car miscalculated or when the leading car's spinout got out of control.

So there was no question the tactic was perilous, even in the hands of an experienced driver. Is that what Jack was counting on? Johnny's inexperience? Was he playing him for a fool? It seemed like a heartless calculation.

"Mind if I ask a question?"

"Fire away," Jack responded.

"You said yourself this is your last race, and I think it's pretty clear there's no love lost between us—"

"Speak for yourself."

"So why are you telling me how to beat you?"

Jack glanced down at his folded hands for a moment, before looking up. When he did there was sadness in his eyes.

"Because it's natural for a father to want to pass something on to his son. Because…it's my way of showing you you're important to me, more important than my own ego."

He rose and stood in place. "There's a lot more I want to say to you, Johnny." He paused as if he were considering enumerating them. "But they'll have to wait until you're ready to hear them. In the meantime—" another pause "—thanks for listening."

He turned and ambled to the door. Johnny remained seated and watched his father let himself out of the motor home. No goodbye. No offer of good luck. He just stepped outside and closed the door behind him.

"Is he gone?"

Johnny spun around and saw Amber standing in the doorway to the bedroom wearing a tank top and short shorts.

"What the hell are you doing here?"

"I came by to see if you might like company tonight. I mean, with the big race tomorrow—"

"How did you get in here?"

"I know the security code, silly." She bit her lip, embarrassed by her smart-mouthed comeback.

"I don't like people spying on me, Amber. You had no right to listen in on my private conversation."

"I didn't mean to, honey. Really. I was about to tell you I was here, when he came to the door, and I didn't think that would be a good time for me to make an appearance."

"So you eavesdropped."

"Johnny, it's not like the two of you were whispering." She was getting upset now. "What did you expect me to do, stick my fingers in my ears?"

He muttered some phrases. If asked a second later he couldn't have said if they were in English or Italian. It didn't make any difference. She understood enough to know he wasn't happy with her.

"Are you going to do it?" she asked.

"You must think I'm as stupid as he does."

"So it's a trick," she concluded, as if that had been her assessment, as well.

"Of course it's a trick. He'd be crazy to let me get behind him long enough to establish a draft, especially if, as he claims, we'll already be in the lead. All he'd have to do is tap his brakes and instead of bumping him I'd rear-end him." Except he'd end up crashing, too, wouldn't he? "No—" he shook his head angrily "—he's not trying to help me, he's trying to sabotage me, set me up." But how? Maybe he ought to talk to Mac or Steiner about this in the morning. "Probably have one of his buddies do a number on my tail while I'm concentrating on his."

"That's mean," Amber said.

"What the hell would you expect from him?"

"So what are you going to do?"

"I'll figure something out."

Amber brushed up against him and clasped her fingers behind his neck. "I know you will." She started to kiss him on the lips.

"No, Amber." He reached up and, fighting his natural impulses, removed her hands. "I told you I didn't want to see you. You shouldn't have come here."

"You don't want me to stay? You want me to leave?" She seemed shocked he was turning her down. He'd never done that before.

"I asked you to stop using drugs. You didn't. Now please leave."

MARGARET ALWAYS SPENT the night before a race at her hotel, rather than at Jack's motor home. She had good reasons. One was his erratic schedule immediately before a race. Another was the unpredictability of the press— no sense in giving them grist for the gossip mill. Finally there was Jack's need for a decent night's sleep, something neither of them was likely to get with her there.

She also always made it a point to let her daughter know specifically where she was staying. Amber never showed up. No matter. It was the principle of the thing. So Margaret was stunned when Amber appeared at her hotel room door the night before the Miami race.

She put on the carafe of water to heat for tea while she listened to her daughter's disappointment about Johnny not wanting her to spend the night with him. Margaret knew Amber was leaving something out but she wouldn't push. When the time was right Amber would tell her what was really going on. Instead Amber reported that Jack had come to see Johnny that evening. Margaret's head shot up.

"Jack was there?"

"That's what I just told you, Mom. Haven't you been listening?"

"Tell me everything that happened. What did they talk about?"

Amber rolled her eyes, then settled into a recitation of the men's conversation, a recounting Margaret suspected was probably pretty accurate, if not verbatim.

Jack had told Johnny how to beat him tomorrow. Amber repeated Johnny's claim that it was a trap, a trick, a sneaky way to humiliate him, but Margaret knew it wasn't. Jack would never do anything to hurt his son.

What was it Amber had just said? The part about it being natural for a father to want to pass something on to his son, that his son was more important to him than his own ego sounded so much like Jack.

After all these months it still surprised her Johnny hadn't reconsidered his opinion of the man. Jack had always been complimentary when talking about him. You'd think Jack's reputation within the NASCAR community would count for something, too, but Johnny seemed determined not to have his mind changed.

Margaret couldn't keep silent any longer. Not when

Jack had offered the only thing he had left, his last victory, the NASCAR NEXTEL Cup Championship, and Johnny was rejecting it.

Jack wouldn't be pleased with what she was about to do, but she had to do it.

"Come with me," she ordered her daughter.

Amber stared at her. "Where are we going?"

"To see Johnny."

"Oh, no, we're not." She backed away, palms upraised in front of her. "He wants to be alone to think. He's going to be really mad if we show up."

"Too bad. He'll get over it. What I have to say you both need to hear. Let's go."

"M-o-m," Amber moaned.

"Amber, let's go."

JACK KEPT REVIEWING his meeting with Johnny. It was only the second conversation they'd had, and he wasn't sure the first one counted.

Would his son heed his advice? He suspected not. The kid was blinded by a mind-set that would have been justified had the underlying premises been true. But, of course, he didn't know they weren't.

Margaret argued that Jack ought to spell out what had really happened twenty-five years ago. The trouble was Johnny wouldn't believe him, not with the kind of brain-washing he'd been subjected to. As for the diaries, maybe she was right. There was a lot to be said for allowing Johnny to read them. The boy would learn the truth, but at what price? Destroying his good impressions of Lillah wouldn't earn Jack any thanks, and

Johnny would still have every right to despise Jack for his weakness, for being a cuckold and for failing to demand custody of his son. In the end Jack would have betrayed Lillah in the eyes of her son for nothing.

Better let him keep his fond memories of her, Jack concluded, even if they are falsely based. He was glad Margaret had destroyed them.

He ought to get some sleep. Tomorrow was going to be a big day, an important day. A milestone. A turning point. How would he measure success? By winning the NASCAR NEXTEL Cup Championship? Or by losing it?

THE NIGHT BEFORE A RACE was always hectic at the track. Late arrivals competing for space with those who had been there for days. Tailgate parties. Barbecues. Friends meeting friends. Families mingling with families.

Margaret got on the long line to the infield, pulled up to the security guard and showed her pass. Amber was required to show hers, as well. Finally she moved forward, drove down to the motor home parking lot. At the far end of the second row she parked and opened her door. Amber didn't move.

"Come on," Margaret commanded.

"He's going to be frosted, I tell you."

"Amber come with me or stay here. At this point I really don't care, but if you stay here you're going to miss out on something very important."

"Why won't you tell me what it is?"

"Because what I have to say isn't for you, it's for Johnny, but I think you should hear it."

Amber weighed her options, tugged on the door

handle and climbed out of the car. She didn't want to miss anything. Margaret clicked the locks shut.

They walked toward the motor homes in silence. Margaret hoped Jack didn't choose that moment to make an appearance. He didn't. She and her daughter walked past his luxury motor home and mounted the steps to his son's.

She rapped on the door more forcefully than her customary polite tap.

No response.

She knocked again, harder this time. Finally she pounded on the door and called out his name, giving her own.

The door opened. Johnny peered at her, irritated at being disturbed, even more vexed when he saw Amber standing behind her mother.

"What do you want?" he demanded, not his usual courteous self.

"We need to talk."

"This isn't a good time."

"It's the only time," she declared.

He crooked an eyebrow, glanced again at Amber, who shrugged her ignorance, and looked once more at the older woman. "What's going on?"

"Let us in."

He hesitated a moment, then stepped aside.

Margaret went to the center of the living area, turned and faced him, then waved her hand toward the couch and told him to sit down.

He gave her the eye, unused to being ordered about in his own home, expecting it least of all from this woman.

"Please sit down," she said, but it was still more a command than a request.

With a bewildered shake of his head he complied, clearly only to humor her. Amber sat next to him and attempted to hold his hand, but he ignored it and she folded hers in her lap. He waved Margaret to the easy chair at the end of the coffee table.

She ignored it and remained standing in front of him.

"I understand Jack was here."

"Amber has a big mouth."

"He gave you some advice."

"He thinks I'm a sucker."

"And I think you're a fool."

"M-o-m," Amber singsonged, wide-eyed.

Johnny stared up in shock, uncertain how to react. "What did you say?"

"I said you're a fool."

It took about five seconds for him to go from flabbergasted to seething. She could see the anger in the set of his jaw and the sharpness of his eyes, but he considered himself a gentleman. He would refrain from reacting with her the way he would if the same words had been spoken by a man.

He rose to his feet. "I think you had better leave."

She didn't budge from her spot. "You think Jack abused your mother and abandoned you."

He said nothing.

"Antonio lied to you, Johnny."

"I want you to leave." He put his hand out as though to guide her to the door. "Now."

Her heart was pounding, but she knew he wouldn't

touch her. She stood firm in spite of the sudden weakness in her knees, even when he was within arm's reach of her.

"Your mother walked out on him, Johnny, after she'd cheated on him with Antonio. Jack tried to go after you, but they wouldn't let him see you, and he didn't have the resources at the time to challenge them legally."

The words were coming out too fast, all run together, but now that she'd started, she didn't seem to know how to stop them or even slow them down.

"The last thing he wanted," she added, "was for you to become a pawn in an international custody battle."

Johnny took a step back and crossed his arms over his chest. He was a big man, and standing this close he was definitely imposing. "Of course that's what he would say."

In spite of her sense of frustration Margaret refused to be intimidated. She just hoped her shaking legs didn't give out on her.

"Do you remember your mother's diaries?" she asked.

The shift in subjects had him pulling back even farther. "Yes," he replied, clearly confused.

"She gave them to me before she died and asked me to read them. I have. What Antonio told you about the situation was a pack of lies."

"That's not true," he objected, but he wasn't as confident as he had been.

"Can we sit down?" she asked. She almost added please.

It took what seemed like an eternity for the request to register, then he waved her to the chair he'd offered her earlier. This time she accepted it.

CHAPTER TWENTY

MARGARET SPENT the next two hours reviewing the events and personalities of three decades earlier. She started with what she felt was probably the beginning, her own friendship with Lillah, then her going steady with Jack.

"How long were you together?" Amber asked.

"Two years. Our sophomore and junior years in high school."

"So what happened? Did he get abusive or something?"

Margaret shook her head. "Jack was never abusive."

"Not with you maybe," Johnny said. "But you don't know about how he was with other women, with my mother."

"He never abused Lillah, Johnny. I knew Jack back then, and I know him now. He would never strike a woman." Then she added, "Any more than you would." The statement caught him by surprise. Subtly he nodded and looked away.

"So why did you break up with him, Mom?"

"I met your father." Margaret had decided to put as positive a face on her relationship with Gary as she could. "He was a fantastic jazz musician, and he…just swept me off my feet."

"Daddy was good, wasn't he?" The note of sadness in Amber's voice broke Margaret's heart. Her little girl really did love her father.

"He was the greatest, honey." For a moment Margaret's throat closed and her eyes began to water. She swallowed a world of regret and went on. "Anyway, I left Jack for him, and my best friend, Lillah, started going out with Jack."

"Did he love her?" Amber asked.

"Not then, but she was giving him what I hadn't—"

"You mean the two of you weren't having sex?"

Margaret felt her face grow warm.

Amber looked at her with amusement. "Gee, Mom, it's no big deal."

"It used to be." This wasn't the kind of subject she wanted to discuss with her daughter, especially in front of the girl's boyfriend. "Anyway, a couple of months after graduation Lillah announced she was pregnant, and Jack did what in those days was considered the honorable thing, he married her."

"So what Larry Waring reported, that Jack had to marry her was true?" Amber asked.

Margaret nodded. "Lillah was pregnant with you," she told Johnny.

He listened, apparently unaffected.

"It wasn't an easy marriage," she continued. "Jack was still racing short track in those days and working a series of part-time jobs to support the family. There wasn't much money and Lillah always had expensive tastes, but they were getting by. They were doing all right. Until they went to Indianapolis."

Margaret's mouth was getting dry and she would have liked a drink of water, but she didn't want to interrupt her narrative.

"That's where she met Antonio, who was touring the States at the time. He was handsome and famous and *rich*." She emphasized the last quality. "Lillah was a beautiful woman, and he told her so. Called her *cara* and *bellissima*."

Amber shot an inquiring glance at Johnny, who sat quietly, staring into space.

"Lillah was smitten. They started meeting behind Jack's back. Color him naive. He'd agree. The truth is he didn't realize what was going on until it was too late, until she'd taken you and flown to Italy."

Johnny squirmed, uncomfortable with this narrative. He probably wanted to object, but to what? Having an affair with a married woman wasn't out of character for the man he'd grown up with.

"Antonio told you Jack never tried to find you or come after you," Margaret told him. "That's simply not true. He borrowed money and flew to Italy. He was determined to bring you home, but the Rendisis turned him away, denied knowing anything about Lillah or you and said Antonio was on the Grand Prix circuit in Australia and then in Asia. Your mother knew Jack would come after you. She also knew Antonio had the resources for them to stay one step ahead of him. She purposely got her divorce in Europe because she knew Jack didn't have the money or connections to successfully contest it there."

"You're making this up."

"Why would I do that, Johnny?"

He took a deep breath and looked away without answering.

"Jack was going crazy trying to find you, to get custody of you, but there was no way he could fight the powerful Rendisis in their own court. Your mother knew that, too, and she took advantage of it. It was years before she fully appreciated the pain she'd caused him, but by then it was too late. Antonio had legally adopted you, and he wasn't about to let you go."

Johnny shot up. "I don't believe any of this," he said, but there was doubt in his voice.

"Don't you? Think about it," Margaret urged, "and think about the personalities involved. I liked your mother at the end, but I also knew her in her earlier days. Two very different people. I'm sure some of the change had to do with the fact that she was dying, but I also know from talking with her and reading her diaries that in the intervening years she did a lot of soul-searching and came to realize how much she'd hurt not just herself and Jack, but you, too."

"She didn't hurt me."

"She took you away from your father. She gave you to a man who was even more selfish and manipulative than she was."

"Antonio was my father." The words were spoken with sulky defiance.

In a flash of insight, Margaret saw the battle that had been raging inside him over his allegiance to a man who hadn't been worthy of it. A boy needs a father, and Johnny had transferred his love to the man his mother, in her vanity and greed, had chosen to fill the role.

"I never met him," she confessed. "From everything I've heard about him he was an interesting, intelligent and charming man. But he also cheated on your mother. You know that. You had to bring his body home from the bed of his mistress."

He glared at her, his jaw muscles working furiously, not pleased at being reminded.

"I'm not going to argue with you about Antonio's character," Margaret went on, "except to say you either recognize cheating on your wife with a series of mistresses is inherently wrong and not the actions of an honorable man, or you don't. If you don't, please tell Amber that soon so she can find someone else to shack up with."

"Mother," Amber exclaimed in horror.

Margaret ignored her. She'd never been this blunt, this bold. She wasn't pleased with the pain she was causing, but there was no way around it.

"What I am here to tell you is that Jack Dolman has never stopped loving you. Yes, he gave you up, but he did so to protect you."

"Mom, that doesn't make sense."

Margaret continued to address Johnny. "He didn't want you to be an international ping-pong, bouncing from one continent to another, being used to hurt other people. He knew your mother loved you, and he had to take the chance that Antonio would treat you well. To make sure, he hired an international detective agency to keep an eye on you."

Another shock, but this time Johnny didn't challenge her.

"Jack came to you tonight and offered you the only

thing he has left. His final victory. You can accept his gift or not. If you do, you'll know he is an honorable man. If you don't, you'll never know. The choice is yours."

She rose from the chair and again stood in front of him. "After the race, I'll give you your mother's diaries, and you can read them." Her voice was soft and sympathetic. "But first you must decide for yourself what you're going to do."

She moved to the door. "Amber, you coming with me?"

"Can I stay here?" she asked Johnny.

"Would you mind waiting outside for a few minutes?" Johnny asked Margaret. "I need to talk to Amber alone, then she'll be leaving with you."

Amber looked crushed. Margaret was equally surprised, but she could hardly refuse.

"Good luck in the race tomorrow," she said and left, closing the door behind her.

"ARE YOU SLEEPING with somebody else, Johnny? Is that what you want to tell me?"

He spun around. "What? No, of course not. When would I?"

That wasn't the answer Amber was seeking. "Would you, if you had the chance?"

The question annoyed him. He had other things on his mind. "I don't sleep around."

"Antonio did, and you want to be just like him."

"Forget about Antonio. He has nothing to do with this."

She regarded him skeptically.

"Here's the deal, Amber," he continued, determined to get at least this issue resolved. "I don't want you the way you are." He watched her eyes go wide, not with anger but with hurt and fear. "So you have a choice. Change, get your act together, or go your own way."

"What…what are you talking about, Johnny?"

"You're a beautiful girl, Amber, one of the most beautiful girls I've ever met. But you're not a woman. You're smart and talented, but you're hiding your intelligence and your talent behind drugs. I don't find that appealing. What's more, as long as you're abusing substances, you're a liability to me, and I can't afford that."

"You've found somebody else." Her eyes filled with tears. "You're using this as an excuse to dump me."

He shook his head the way an adult would toward a willful child.

"There's no one else, Amber." He lowered his voice to a sympathetic murmur. "But at this point I don't like you very much. You can change that, and I hope you do, because I care for you. I mean that. I care for you a lot, but not the way you are. I'm not sure if we have a chance together. I'd like to find out. All I know is that it's over between us if you don't get help and stay clean."

"You're just worried about your precious career."

"You're absolutely correct, and I'm not making any apologies for that. I am worried about my career. I have prospects for a good life ahead of me, and I'm not going to blow it on a junkie. Look—" he reached out and held her shoulders at arm's length "—I'm willing to help you. I want to. I'll send you someplace where they can help you, and I'll pay all the bills, all the expenses for as long as it takes. But you have to want to change, to get better."

"You'd do that for me?" Suddenly she was a little girl again.

"I told you I care about you. I want you to get better, Amber. I want you to be the charming, sophisticated young woman I met in Europe. But my help isn't unconditional. You blow it, and you're on your own."

"And when I come back we'll be together again?" The plea for hope in her voice was heartbreaking, and he wanted desperately to say yes, but lying would only make matters worse. Besides, lies had a way of catching up with you.

"I don't know, Amber. I can't promise we will. Who knows, when you get clean you may not want me."

"I'll always want you, Johnny. Always."

He hoped it was her insecurities talking, because that kind of unconditional hero worship was scary and dangerous.

"You say that now, but you may not later," he said. "Let's give it time. Okay?"

"I'll do anything you want. You know that."

This wasn't exactly working out the way he'd envisioned, but it was better than an outright refusal to get help. And God help him, he was afraid he really did love her, or at least the mature, lovable woman she sometimes was.

"I'll talk to your mom, and we'll work out the details."

"Anything you say, Johnny. You just tell me what you want me to do." She tried to kiss him, but he gently held her off.

MARGARET WAITED until they were back at the hotel before she finally asked Amber what Johnny had wanted to talk to her about.

"He wants me to go into rehab."

So he's finally had enough, too.

"He said he would pay for everything, for as long as it takes."

"That's very generous of him. Are you going to accept his offer?"

"He won't take me back if I don't."

So he was gambling on tough love, too. Was it only a game he was playing? She hoped not. It came down, she supposed, to which father he chose to emulate. Antonio Rendisi or Jack Dolman.

"I think I'll take a shower," Amber said and marched into the bedroom.

The suite Jack had booked for her had two queen-size beds. Margaret parked herself on the one near the window. A few minutes later Amber emerged from the bathroom wearing one of the terry cloth bathrobes supplied by the luxury hotel.

"Let's talk," Margaret said.

Amber screwed up her face. "About what?" She climbed onto the other bed, modestly pulled the robe around her legs and hugged her knees.

"I'm glad Johnny is willing to send you to rehab, and I'm really happy you're going to accept, but I also wish you'd tell me what you've been taking and why. What's really bothering you, sweetheart? What are you afraid of?"

"Why do you think I'm afraid of something?"

"Because that's why people abuse substances, because they're afraid to face reality. I want so much to help you, but I can't if you won't tell me what's troubling you."

Amber stretched out on the other bed, her head on the pillows, her hands folded at her waist.

"You haven't figured it out, have you? I was so sure you would, then you'd take the pills away."

Pills. Margaret had never heard of birth control pills having nearly psychotic effects on a patient. Didn't mean it couldn't happen, but why only since they'd returned to the States? "Amber, please tell me what's going on."

Her daughter took a breath, let it out. "It's the pain, Mom. I'm afraid of the pain."

A chill ran down Margaret's spine. Endometriosis. It was back. More surgery, only this time it would have to be radical. Her heart sank.

"You're in pain? That's why you've been taking drugs? Oh, honey."

She remembered the agony her daughter had endured when she'd had the first episode, how she'd spent days crying, doubled up in tears.

"When did it start?"

"It hasn't," Amber explained impatiently, "but I'm afraid it will. That's why I've been taking the pills." Her tone changed to one of confusion. "But they're doing funny things."

"What pills, honey?"

"The antidepressants, of course."

Now Margaret was completely baffled. "I don't understand."

Amber had been prescribed antidepressants before

and again after her surgery. But that had been almost three years ago.

"I thought you stopped taking them before we went to Europe."

"I was supposed to start tapering off, but I was scared to. I planned to do it in Europe. I packed them in my cosmetic case, but then... You remember. It got left behind and I had to replace all my makeup and toiletries in Rome—" she smiled "—and Lillah insisted on taking us to that fancy shop where she bought her stuff and paying for everything. That was fun." She beamed at the recollection. The bill had been close to a thousand dollars.

"I got panicky when I realized I didn't have my pills," Amber went on. "The doctor said I shouldn't stop taking them all at once, so I told Lillah's doctor the name of what I'd been prescribed, and he gave me a new prescription so I could get it there. He said I could taper off when I was ready."

"He gave you medication without my permission?" Margaret was furious. Amber had been underage. In this country, anyway. Maybe the same rules didn't apply over there. "You were taking them the whole time we were in Italy?"

Amber nodded. "But my last refill ran out right after we came home, so I've been taking the ones I had left over from before."

"You've been taking expired psychotropic pills? Oh, my God, Amber."

"They were perfectly all right, Mom. They were still in the cosmetic case, right where I'd left it in my closet."

It was finally beginning to make sense. Margaret

went over and sat on the side of Amber's bed and took one of her hands.

"Sweetheart," she said patiently, "there's a reason they put dates on drugs. After a while some of them just lose their potency, but others go bad."

She gathered her daughter in her arms and hugged her. Teary-eyed with relief, she said, "I thought you were taking illegal narcotics, when all you were taking was outdated medication."

"You mean I won't have to go to rehab?"

"I don't know. We'll have to find out."

"I'll go if you…and Johnny want me to."

Margaret gave her daughter another hug. For the first time in months she felt she was getting her daughter back.

"Now this pain you're worried about," she said. "Are you or aren't you experiencing any?"

Amber shook her head. "But I'm afraid I will. I don't want to have surgery, Mom. I don't want them cutting me up inside, ruining me. I want to have children like other women."

And I want to be a grandmother someday.

Another thought entered Margaret's mind, one that didn't please her one bit—and definitely wouldn't please Johnny.

"You haven't stopped taking the birth control pills, have you? You're not trying to get pregnant?"

Amber avoided eye contact. "I thought about it," she admitted. "I figured if he knew I was going to have his baby…" She heaved a big sigh. "No, Mom. I'm not trying to get pregnant. I'm still taking the pill."

Margaret relaxed marginally. "That's good. Please don't stop."

"Johnny's not going to marry me, anyway. He told me tonight he doesn't like me."

It was hard not to smile. "I don't think that's true, honey. He's offered to send you to rehab. I don't think he'd do that if he didn't like you. He's been worried about you, just like I have."

Margaret grasped Amber's hands and tugged on them, forcing her to look at her mother. "He does care about you. Do you care for him?"

"I love him, Mom."

Margaret was relieved to hear the words weren't spoken breezily but with sincerity.

Love was full of so many contradictions. It was delicate, yet so powerful. So fragile, yet it imbued such strength. It was like a drug that didn't expire with time, yet had such terrible consequences when it went bad. She believed her daughter really did love Johnny. She just hoped she wouldn't be hurt by that love.

CHAPTER TWENTY-ONE

FOR JOHNNY THE MIAMI RACE didn't start well. Having won the pole, he was able to hold on to the lead for the first six laps, but then a blowout by a car behind him caused a major pileup that brought out the caution flag. Another six laps went by in slow motion. When the all-clear came Johnny was still in front, but the interruption had given other drivers opportunities to work out strategies and negotiate deals. By the second lap after resumption of the race, Rafael O'Bryan was drafting with Crane Dawkins, and the two slipped past Johnny. They were followed by Jem Nordstrom and Haze Clifford.

Johnny put in a hurried call for help, which was answered by Jack Dolman, who quickly fell in behind him and immediately formed a draft.

Johnny was torn. The man he said he hated, the man who the night before had insisted he wanted to help him, was now in a position to really hurt him, maybe even end his race. Except that a bump at this point would probably terminate Jack's race, too, since they were in such close quarters, and a spinout immediately in front of him would inevitably catch Jack in its chaos.

Accepting fate and the push he received from the

Number 424 car, Johnny slipped to the right, past Numbers 487 and 541. They were abreast of Clifford and Nordstrom now. Then Mitch Volmer pulled up on Jack's tail, completing a longer draft. Suddenly Johnny felt himself speed up still more. Inch by inch he nosed ahead of Nordstrom.

"Go for it," Mac said in his ear.

Johnny didn't need a second invitation. He shot to the left, ahead of Nordstrom. As he did so he lost his draft and instantly slowed, which exposed him to a bump by Nordstrom, either intentionally or by accident. Johnny had to count on the man's skill and experience. From his inside, locked position, Nordstrom would be the first casualty in a spinout.

Nordstrom wisely slowed to maintain a safe distance, at least for the moment.

As Johnny fell into place ahead of him, Jack stayed in his draft with Mitch Volmer in the outside lane. Together they were pulling ahead of Johnny. A draft at this point with Nordstrom would give Johnny the advantage and allow him to reestablish the lead, but by the time he felt the push from behind, his father and Volmer had gained a car length.

Suddenly Johnny was in the position Nordstrom had been in only seconds before. He had no choice but to cede his number one position. For the moment. He had to hand it to his old man. By having Johnny pull in front of Nordstrom, Jack had made him directly and solely vulnerable. By maintaining the draft with Volmer and letting the trailing car come into the number two spot, Jack had put Johnny in third place.

Slick move, old man. I'll remember that.

Jack held first place for the next twenty laps, until he had to come in for a pit stop. Mac called Johnny in at the same time.

Johnny shot onto pit road right behind the Number 424 car. Jack pulled into his space. A second later Johnny halted three spaces ahead in his. Gas and tire change for each took less than fourteen seconds. Within thirty seconds from the time they'd entered pit road, they were both back on the track, fighting to regain their former positions at the front of the lead pack.

The rest of the race had the usual distractions. A car near the end of the trailing pack blew an engine, spewing oil across the roadway and sending the caution flag up for half a dozen laps. Later a car lost a wheel, spun out and bounced off the wall, causing a major pileup that eliminated four other cars. Another driver lost control, got sideswiped, rolled three times and ended up unharmed in the grass.

By the last ten laps, a total of twelve cars had been eliminated. This was as competitive a race as Johnny had ever experienced.

Jack was in first place. Jem Nordstrom held second. Johnny in third. The last pit stop had been completed. The crowd was in a frenzy.

Johnny had discussed strategies with Mac and Steiner before the race. He hadn't told them about Jack's visit the evening before, but he had presented the scenario of someone being in front of him in the last lap of the race. The two older, more experienced men agreed a bump-draft was the tactic to use. Steiner had also voiced his concern that Johnny was afraid of it—he used the word uncomfortable—and strongly suggested he get over it.

"Time to move up," Mac said now into his headset.

Johnny knew what that meant. The question was whether Nordstrom would let him get close enough to give him the bump? He doubted it. Nordstrom was not only a very skilled driver, but a greedy one.

The obvious game now was leapfrogging. The trailing two cars would draft past the first, then the new trailing pair would leap in front of the new leader. They would keep the pattern up for as long as they could till the last lap.

The number three car always had an incentive to offer a draft because the resulting slingshot pass would bring him into the number two position and put him in position to bump the lead.

The number two car had only one incentive to give the leader a draft—to bump him. For that reason, whoever was in the lead would be constantly maneuvering back and forth, both to prevent a bump-draft and to block, but every time he moved to protect himself from one of his followers, he was vulnerable to being passed by the other.

It was a constant game of cat and mouse, except in this case the fleeing mouse had two cats toying with him—nerve-racking, split-second timing in close quarters at 180-plus miles an hour. Nothing matched the excitement.

Nordstrom, in second place, was smart enough to know coming in second was better than being wiped out, so he protected his rear by lurching from side to side, not enough to significantly slow him down, but enough to keep Johnny from establishing the draft he needed to bump him out of the competition. Meanwhile, Jack continued down the track in the lead.

The three of them weren't the only ones on the track, of course. Just behind Johnny was Rafael O'Bryan, and following him was the first pack, desperately maneuvering for whatever positions they could sabotage. O'Bryan had lost a lap when he'd had to pull off the track with a tire problem half a dozen laps back and hadn't been able to make it up.

Would he be willing to play spoiler against Nordstrom? Johnny had Mac ask.

"Against Nordstrom? You bet."

Jem, it seemed, hadn't made himself many friends over the past few seasons. Cutthroat tactics had a way of coming back to bite a guy.

Johnny drifted to the right. O'Bryan glided up behind him. Nordstrom, savvy to what was happening, eased slightly to the right, but he couldn't go too far to the outside without leaving himself open on the inside.

They circled through Turns Three and Four. Johnny refused to give ground on the outside. They hit the straightaway and Johnny leaped forward, Rafael on his tail.

Without a push, Nordstrom couldn't match the speed. Johnny was sorely tempted to move in front of his competitor, but remembering the lesson he'd learned from his father, he pressed on, lost a few feet in Turn One, a few more in Turn Two, but was still a nose ahead.

On the backstretch he went high and gunned it.

O'Bryan stuck to his bumper. The two of them shot ahead, pulling to the left as they hit Turn Three, into the void between Jack and Jem.

Visually Nordstrom was now in fourth place, never mind that O'Bryan was officially a lap behind him. He remained an obstacle to be overtaken, eliminated, if Nordstrom was going to take the lead.

Three laps to go. Jack was still out in front.

How the hell had he known it would play out this way? Johnny asked himself. He wasn't prone to conspiracy theories, but if he were, this would be close to the top of the list.

Jack in the lead. Johnny in second. O'Bryan in the third position but not a contender for the checkered flag.

If he and Jack had conspired, however, Rafael could wipe Johnny out!

Johnny doubted it. Rafe was an honest man.

Funny, yesterday he wouldn't have said the same thing for Jack, but now the notion didn't seem so outrageous.

In his rearview mirror, Johnny saw Nordstrom cut to the inside and slingshot around O'Bryan. Damn that put Nordstrom on Johnny's tail. Double damn.

Okay, Johnny told himself, *he's still two car lengths behind me.* A decent margin.

Nobody was drafting now. Everybody was evenly paced.

Two laps.

Suddenly, in his rearview mirror, Johnny saw O'Bryan zoom up behind Nordstrom, ram his bumper, and within seconds the two cars were playing spin the bottle, one behind the other.

Had it been intentional on O'Bryan's part?

Had it been preplanned or merely opportunistic? No telling at this point.

The pack, which had been bulleted immediately behind the two was now in disarray and quickly fading into the distance. Johnny stared through his windshield.

Like you said, Jack. It's just you and me.

MARGARET WASN'T SURE she was going to survive the day. This was by far the most intense and exciting race she'd ever witnessed.

She'd tossed and turned the night before after Amber fell asleep, trying to decide how Jack would react when he found out she'd violated their agreement not to tell Johnny about the diaries. He wouldn't be pleased. She wasn't, either. But would he understand? All she felt was heart-pounding, palm-sweating rushes of adrenaline as she watched cars darting back and forth, trading leads, maneuvering for advantages that seemed to evaporate as quickly as they materialized.

Jack had told Johnny the contest would be between the two of them in the last lap. He'd been uncannily right. He'd also told his son it would be up to him to eliminate his father if he really wanted to win.

Win. Margaret wasn't sure she even understood the concept anymore.

Her heart stopped as she watched Rafe O'Bryan clip Jem Nordstrom, then the two of them spin out in slow graceful rotations until the pack caught up with them and sparks began to fly. But she wasn't interested in them. She shifted her attention to the two cars ahead of them. To the green-and-yellow car, Number 424, driven by Jack Dolman, and the black-and-silver car immediately behind it, Number 581, driven by his son, Johnny Rendisi.

CHAPTER TWENTY-TWO

TWO LAPS TO GO. Nordstrom out of the picture. O'Bryan, as well. Six car lengths separating Johnny from his closest trailing competitor. Jack crowding his windshield.

The last lap will be ours. If you really want to win, there's only one way to do it. You're going to have to get on my butt, establish a draft and bump me.

Crunch time.

They went into Turn One. Jack in the lead, Johnny half a length behind him.

Turn Two. The same.

The backstretch. Jack hugged the inside until Johnny moved closer, then slipped right far enough to evade him. Johnny followed. Jack tightened to the left in time to take Turn Three.

Turn Four.

The frontstretch. The white flag signaling the last lap.

Johnny's already taut muscles ached. His breathing stopped. His heart thudded. They were *this close*. *He* was this close.

Turn One. Johnny rode Jack's bumper for a split second, but Jack maneuvered just enough to prevent a draft.

Turn Two was over in tenths of a second.

The backstretch. Now was the time.

All or nothing.

Go for broke.

Do it.

Johnny crowded the car in front of him, but Jack continued to weave enough to avoid a slipstream. Johnny moved up tighter. He only needed a second. One second.

Turn Three was coming up fast.

Ride his butt. But Jack weaved from side to side.

Turn Four. Touch.

Except Jack had anticipated it and was already moving to the right to counter the effect.

Out of the last turn. Jack shimmied back and forth.

Do it, dammit.

As Jack hugged the inside, Johnny rode tight up on his bumper and touched him again. Harder this time.

Jack's tail began a slow drift to the right as they charged onto the homestretch. Not totally out of control. Jack was too good to let that happen, but he had to move right.

The inside lane was clear. Johnny mashed the pedal to the floor with enough pressure to break through the fire wall. His hands maintained a death grip on the wheel—as if that would make the car go faster.

Suddenly he was on the inside, beside Jack. No time to look over.

Press the metal. Inch forward.

In the corner of his eye he caught a glimpse of Jack's car regaining forward momentum, but at the cost of speed.

Ahead the checkered flag.

His father was lost in Johnny's blind spot, some-where behind him.

Johnny crossed the finish line, the checkered flag waving furiously above him.

Johnny Rendisi had taken the NASCAR NEXTEL Cup Championship.

He'd achieved what he set out to do. He'd denied *his father* victory. His last victory.

Johnny had won.

Or had he?

JOHNNY'S RIGHT LEG was shaking as he let up on the gas pedal. He approached the first turn. The cars behind him did, too. On the next lap the others would file onto pit road, leaving the track to him, then he'd be handed the checkered flag to drive his official victory lap. This was cooling-down time, a chance to get his heart to stop hammering like a steam locomotive chugging uphill.

The car was a sweatbox. He was drenched with per-spiration. His arm muscles quivered in spite of the iron-fisted grip he had on the wheel. From the backstretch he could see the frantic writhing in the stands, sense rather than hear the roar of the crowds.

He coasted through Turns Three and Four. Elements of the pack were in front of him, making their way off the field, giving it all to him. One car was easing its way down from the outside bank toward pit road.

Johnny slammed on his brakes in front of it.

His father raised his visor, looked squarely at him, a quizzical expression on his face.

Johnny couldn't hear his words over the thrum and

beat of engines and cheering people, but he could read his lips. *Congratulations. You did it.*

Now everything went into slow motion. The expression on his father's face shone with the radiance of a saint in one of those medieval paintings Italy was famous for. But this was a real man, and in Jack's blue eyes Johnny saw selfless pride. It felt good and it hurt at the same time.

Johnny had spent the night searching memories, trying to piece together the kaleidoscope of his life. *Consider the personalities involved,* Margaret had urged. Johnny had thought about how his mother had changed over the years, slowly evolving from a laughing, madcap mommy to an introspective, indulgently smiling but strangely sad mother, even before her husband had died in another woman's bed.

He'd stared at the back of the chair where he'd draped the quilt Margaret had given him, and suddenly he experienced the sensation of lying in a bed in a little boy's room and it being tenderly pulled up to his chin. It hadn't been in a dusty attic all these years he now realized. His father had kept it.

Jack continued to roll to pit road. Johnny pulled up beside him.

"Join me," he called out.

Jack's head shot up. "What?"

"This one's for you, Dad. Join me."

The confusion, the wonder, the sudden appearance of tears in Jack's startled eyes, Johnny decided, was worth it all.

Jack climbed out of his car, walked over to Johnny's

passenger side window and leaned over. Johnny extended his hand, smiled, and without a word they shook hands.

"Sit on the window," Johnny finally said, "and hold on for dear life, old man."

In less time than it would have taken to change four tires and download twenty-two gallons of fuel, Jack Dolman had slung his legs inside the passenger side window, his butt on the frame, his shoulders above the roof.

Johnny did a Polish Victory Lap, driving the track backward, clockwise, his outstretched left arm waving to the crowd. From his unorthodox vantage point Jack was facing them and waving, as well.

Officials were waiting for them when Johnny pulled into Victory Lane. He wouldn't be climbing out of his car, however, until he got the signal that TV cameras were ready to record it for live broadcast. Jack started to extricate himself from the vehicle. Johnny reached across and clasped his leg. Leaning down and over, he made eye contact with his father. "Hang around."

Jack frowned uncertainly. "This is your time, son."

"It's *ours*. Stay with me."

Jack's face took on a strange, unbelieving expression. He nodded and continued to get out of the window but stood at the side of the car, waiting for the TV cameras to roll. If anyone had looked they would have seen his blue eyes were watering.

At the signal, Johnny pulled himself through his window, started to extend his fists above his head, then stopped. He went around the end of the car, grabbed his father's right hand in his left and, grinning from ear to ear, raised them up in the classic victory stance. As cameras clicked he lowered his hands and gave his father a tight hug.

The media crowded around, microphones tipped forward, video cams focused, still cameras clicked and whirred.

"How does it feel to win your first NASCAR NEXTEL Cup Championship?" Larry Waring asked, as he shoved a microphone in Johnny's face.

"Like nothing I've ever experienced before." He put his arm around Jack's shoulder. "Everything I know about winning stock car races I owe to this man."

"So the feud between you is over?" Waring asked.

"What feud?" Johnny presented his best grin.

Johnny could see confusion on the face of the man with the microphone. Had he and the rest of the media been taken in?

Amber and her mother were among the group surrounding them. Johnny signaled them over. To his surprise, Amber didn't coil herself around him the way she had on other occasions. She gave him a chaste peck on the cheek and whispered. "I'm proud of you."

He kissed her back, on the mouth and watched her face light up as he pulled away and smiled at her.

Margaret stood beside Jack and quietly slipped her hand in his.

"What do you think about your son stealing the Cup from you at the very last moment?" Waring asked Jack.

"I'm proud as heck of him. I've had a fantastic career in NASCAR, and now I'm blessed with the opportunity to pass the baton on to my son. What more could a father ask?"

"So you don't feel cheated of this final victory?"

"How can a father possibly feel cheated when he sees his son succeed at what they both love? I can't imagine a better retirement present."

Other interviews followed for both men. Later, though, when Johnny again asked Jack to stay with him, Jack declined. "This is your victory. Enjoy it. Just because I'm not with you, don't think I'm not savoring every bit of it, too. Except for the day you were born, this is the happiest day of my life."

"We need to talk."

"And we will. There's so much I want to say, to tell you, but there'll be plenty of time for that later."

JACK WAS IN A STATE of euphoria as he made his way back to his motor home.

He should be disappointed that he hadn't won the race, but he hadn't been lying when he told the reporter he wasn't. He would have given up all his awards and trophies to have his son back.

He was eager to spend time with Margaret now. She'd been quiet through the awards and interviews, a smile on her lips, looking pleased one moment and almost fearful the next, as if she couldn't believe what was happening.

When things had marginally calmed down, Johnny had gone to her and kissed her on the cheek. Jack was almost certain he'd heard him say thank you to her. Exactly why, he wasn't sure. The general elation of victory that made a man want to thank everyone? Or was there a specific reason?

He unlocked the motor home door and let her precede him inside, then he made sure it was locked behind them. She seemed remarkably shy when he put his arms around her and gave her a big kiss. Well, yes, he did need a shower....

"Join me?" he asked.

She smiled. "Go ahead. I'll wait here."

Her reticence surprised him. It wasn't as if they were exactly strangers to each other.

Twenty minutes later, scrubbed clean and freshly shaven, he rejoined her in the living room. She presented him with an opened bottle of his favorite micro-brewery beer.

"I bet you can use this," she said with a tentative smile.

"Actually I had other refreshment in mind."

She smiled that knowing smile, the one that upped his blood pressure dramatically. When she said nothing in response, he waved the bottle by the neck and asked, "Where's yours?"

"I have wine." She pointed to a glass of white wine. "I'm glad things have finally worked out between you and Johnny."

He tilted his head back, took a long draw on the brew, smacked his lips and grinned. "Yeah, me, too."

"I understand you went to see him last evening."

He glanced over at her. "He told you? When?"

"He didn't. Amber did. She was in his bedroom when you stopped by. She overheard your conversation and came to my hotel room to tell me about it."

He took another pull on his beer. "I really didn't expect him to follow through on my suggestion. I was sure he thought I was trying to trick him."

"He did."

Jack's attention sharpened. Why were they having this conversation and why now, when all he wanted to do was make love?

"Is that what Amber told you?" he asked.

"Can we sit down?"

He saw worry on her face and heard it in her voice.

"Sure." He moved over to the couch, sat down and patted the seat beside him. But instead of snuggling up next to him, as he'd expected, she took the love seat kitty-corner to the sofa. "Is something wrong, Megs?"

"I need to tell you something. Confess."

"I don't like the sound of this," he said lightly, trying to diminish the tension growing between them. "Confess to what?"

"When Amber came over last evening and told me you'd visited Johnny, she said he'd been outraged that you thought he was so stupid he'd take your advice and end up wiping himself out of the race."

"Obviously he thought things through and changed his mind."

"I went to see him."

Eyes still on her, Jack started to take another swig of beer, thought better of it, placed the bottle on the end table and sat back. "Go on."

"I told him about the diaries, Jack."

He crossed his arms. The air between them all but crackled. He said nothing for a long while as he studied her. She accepted his piercing gaze without flinching, but he could see it wasn't easy. At last the strain had him climbing wearily to his feet. He hadn't felt cheated out of the Cup this afternoon, but now Jack had to wonder if Johnny had followed his advice because he'd reached the conclusion on his own that Jack could be trusted, or because the diaries had convinced him of the truth. In the end, he decided, it probably didn't matter. Johnny had taken the advice and now Jack had his son back, which was the important thing.

But had the reunion he'd dreamed of for a quarter of a century come at a price?

"I asked you not to, Margaret. You promised you wouldn't."

Head bowed, she bit her lower lip, but when she looked up, the fire, the strength was still in her eyes.

"I had to, Jack. What he was doing to you was wrong. I had the power to change it."

"You told me you were going to destroy the diaries," he reminded Margaret.

"Yes."

"But you didn't."

"No."

"Why not?"

She hugged herself for a moment before answering. "Because I realized it wouldn't be right. Lillah had passed those diaries on to me for people to see. I should never have offered you a say-so over their disposition."

"But once you did, didn't you feel any obligation to keep your word?"

She turned her head and fixed her gaze on a spot of

the carpet, her mouth pinched. In shame, in frustration, in anger? He couldn't decide.

"I tried talking to you, Jack. Don't you remember? I begged you to let me show them to Johnny, but you were adamant, so I finally just dropped the subject because you were being so damn stubborn." She took a breath. "I knew if I kept fighting you, you'd want me to turn them over to you. Then they would have been destroyed, and I would have failed Lillah. More than that, I would have failed you and Johnny."

"So even after my repeated statements that I didn't want Johnny to see them and in spite of my explanation of why, that I didn't want his mother's memory besmirched, you gave them to him anyway."

"No, Jack, no." Her hazel eyes glimmered with eagerness now, and the words came tumbling out faster. "You don't understand. I haven't given them to him. I told him he could see them after the race, but that he would have to decide for himself first if he really thought you were the villain Antonio made you out to be."

"After the race?" He took a moment to digest this. "You mean he hasn't read them yet?"

She shook her head, her face showing the first signs of relief. "I know you didn't want me to tell him about them, Jack, and I'm sorry I broke my word to you, but I was tired of seeing the two of you tear each other apart when it wasn't necessary, when it was within my power to correct the situation. Lillah gave me those diaries and trusted me to do the right thing with them. I think now I have."

He studied her. Margaret. Megs. Not a girl anymore,

but a mature woman, a woman who challenged and energized him. She'd walked away from him when they were young, and he'd been fool enough to let her. Now she was in effect inviting him to walk away from her again. He'd had flaws back then. God help him, he still did. Always would. But he'd learned something over the years, everybody came with flaws. One thing he was determined about. He wouldn't let her go this time.

He rose, made his way around the corner of the low table and sat beside her, his thigh touching hers. Draping an arm across her shoulders, he tugged her gently to his side. She hesitated but didn't resist, and after a second she snuggled up against him.

Tipping up her chin, he studied her lips, then kissed them, a slow searching indulgence that left them both breathless.

"I should be angry with you," he said a minute later. "You know that?"

She burrowed her head deeper into his shoulder. "I know. I've mishandled this from the start," she said, pressing her hand against his heart, feeling the slow, rhythmic beat. "It's all my fault. Forgive me?"

He shifted enough to meet her eyes and gazed at her so intensely, she felt he was penetrating her soul.

"There's nothing to forgive, Megs," he said softly, solemnly. "You did the right thing. I shouldn't have asked you not to show the diaries to Johnny in the first place. Maybe if I had trusted your judgment, he and I could have been friends all this time."

Cheek against his chest, she could hear his heartbeat, firm and steady.

"I'm not sure that's true," she muttered. "He's been so bitter, so determined to hate you that he might well have rejected the evidence." She looked up. "I think you were right that he needed these months to see you as a real person, a man, not just the caricature Antonio made you out to be. He had to learn to appreciate and trust you on his own. And he has."

He kissed her again, a long, slow, tantalizing sharing that tasted of heat and want and need and had both their blood pressures rising.

"You called me stubborn," he said, when they finally broke off. "You really meant pigheaded, didn't you?"

She smiled for the first time. "Actually, I had a few other terms in mind, as well."

"Maybe I better not ask what they were."

"Good idea." She grinned up at him mischievously. "Stubborn has a nice ring to it, and it's only two syllables."

"Keep it simple, stupid, huh?" He laughed.

She pulled back and looked at him very seriously. "I never said you were stupid, Jack."

He let out a breath. "Good. Because I might get really offended if you did."

"Oh—" she shook her head "—I wouldn't want to offend you."

"What would you like to do?"

She smiled at him and he knew.

CHAPTER TWENTY-THREE

JACK HAD ARRANGED the meeting at his house for eight o'clock Tuesday morning after the race. There would be the four of them, Johnny, Margaret, Amber and himself. Megs prepared a huge mound of scrambled eggs, a pound of bacon, a pot of grits, a stack of biscuits, a pitcher of orange juice, and a backup carafe of coffee, in addition to the fresh pot she was serving from.

"Four people, Megs," he said, brushing her hair away from the side of her face so he could plant a kiss on her temple. "Not four pit crews."

"I don't want anyone to go hungry."

He laughed. "Not a chance."

Everyone was smiling as they poured juice and doctored their coffee to taste. Without makeup, Amber seemed to glow more brilliantly than she did with all the mascara and eye shadow she usually wore. She was quiet this morning, but Jack also felt he was getting a glimpse of the woman her mother had bragged about.

Margaret had told him Sunday night about her daughter's medication problem. Jack, too, had been relieved to learn Amber wasn't using illegal narcotics, though the legal drugs she was taking might well be just as addicting.

"What time did you finally escape the media the other night?" he asked his son, as he refilled his coffee cup.

Johnny continued stacking his plate with breakfast food. "I thought I'd shaken them around eight, but when I went over to the lounge a little after nine another one ambushed me."

Jack snickered. He'd been in that position a few times. It was heartening and annoying at the same time. The press, he'd found over the years, were usually considerate after the initial onslaught, but not always, especially if they thought they had an exclusive on some hot topic.

"Did you get much of a hassle?"

Johnny laughed. "Actually I didn't, then I figured out why. They're still not sure if our *feud* was for real or a publicity stunt, and I think they're a little afraid to find out. I did field a few questions about how we get along."

"What did you tell them?"

He grinned. "I said we got along great, and left it at that. They're still wondering."

Jack laughed. "Smart. Leave them guessing. I'll tell them the same thing."

Margaret prepared herself a plate, and the four of them sat at the rarely used mahogany dining room table.

As they ate, they talked about the upcoming season, about Johnny's prospects, and finally about Jack's retirement plans.

"I talked to Steiner last night," Johnny said. "I know you said you were going to stay on with Sirocco as an advisor, but Steiner says he's willing to negotiate a deal with you about joining my team—if you're interested."

Jack was stunned and moved. Interested? Did anybody really have to ask?

Johnny took a forkful of scrambled eggs. "I'm hoping you'll at least consider it. I know you've been with Sirocco a long time, but…"

"Actually I approached Doug Habersham to see if he might be interested in getting you."

Johnny raised a brow. "Is he?"

Jack chuckled. "You just won the NASCAR NEXTEL Cup Championship, son. What do you think? I'm not sure Steiner will be willing to give you up, though. I sure wouldn't."

Johnny smiled. "Could make for interesting negotiations."

"Profitable, too," Jack added.

They ate in silence for a minute. Margaret got up and started refilling coffee cups.

"There is one other thing I needed to talk to you about," Jack said to his son. He motioned to Margaret, who went to an attaché case on the end of the buffet counter and withdrew three small leather-bound volumes. She passed them to Jack.

He gazed for a moment at the inch-thick, gold-edged books, then offered them to Johnny. "These are your mother's diaries. She gave them to Margaret for safekeeping, but since you're her direct heir, they belong to you."

Johnny held them in his hands, then set them on the table in front of him without bothering to open any of them. "Have you read them?"

Jack shook his head. "Margaret's told me basically what they contain, but I haven't looked at them. Actually, this is the first time I've even seen them."

Johnny pushed them back toward his father. "I don't want them."

"But—"

"She's gone. I know she was a lousy wife to you, but in spite of everything, she was a pretty good mom to me. I'm sorry I wasn't a better son to her. She made mistakes, like the rest of us, but I have no interest in wallowing in her sins."

Jack made no effort to reach for them. "What do you want to do with them then?"

"Keep them. Throw them away. Better yet, burn them. Let's let her rest."

Jack got up and went to the other end of the table. "Stand up."

Bewildered, Johnny did.

"I've been wanting to do this for a long time," Jack said. He threw his arms around his son's shoulders. "I'm proud of you, son. I think she would be, too."

Johnny returned the manly embrace.

Margaret reached for the box of tissues on the counter behind her.

Jack went back to his place and sat down again. Johnny, however, moved to Amber's chair, stood behind it and placed his hands on her shoulders.

"We have an announcement to make," he said. "Thanks to Margaret's frantic efforts yesterday, we've found a rehab center where Amber can go and get a complete medical and psychological evaluation. We don't know at this point how long she'll be there. Maybe only a couple of weeks, maybe longer. But when she returns we're planning to get together—" he gently massaged her shoulders and grinned "—to see if we still like each other."

Amber lowered her head.

Margaret reached for another tissue.

"One other thing," Johnny added. "When she gets back she's also going to try out for the civic symphony."

"Oh, sweetie." Margaret reached for her hand and squeezed it.

Johnny checked his watch. "We need to get going. Her bag is already packed and in the car."

When Amber climbed to her feet, Margaret jumped up and hugged her. A minute later they were both reaching for tissues. Fortunately the box had been a fresh one.

Fifteen minutes later, after more embraces, the young couple was gone.

Margaret was a nervous wreck after they left. She laughed. "I want to say I need a drink, but I don't think it would be appropriate under the circumstances."

Jack raised an eyebrow and grinned. "Especially at nine o'clock in the morning."

"Surely the sun is over the yardarm somewhere," she quipped.

"There's champagne in the fridge. I could fix mimosas with all that orange juice you have left over." He took her in his arms, rubbed her back soothingly. "But I have another idea."

Her eyes twinkled. "Oh, yeah?"

"Marry me."

"What?"

"Marry me, Megs."

"That's what I thought you said."

"Please say yes."

"Okay," she said, feigning nonchalance. "Yes."

He stared at her. "You will? You'll marry me?"

"You did just ask me to, didn't you?"

"Yes, of course, but—"

"Changed your mind already, huh?"

"No. It's just that I forgot to tell you something first."

She continued to gaze at him with amusement. "Uh-oh. I should have known there'd be a glitch. Okay, Mr. NASCAR retiree. What should you have told me first?"

He tightened his embrace and gazed into her eyes. "I love you, Megs. I forgot to tell you I love you."

"Me, too."

He wrinkled his brow.

"I forgot to tell you I love you, too," she said. "And I do love you. I think I always have."

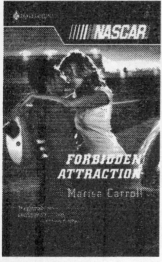

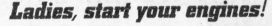